Antonina Irena Brzozowska was born and educated in the north-east of England.

A former teacher, her interests incorporate the Polish, Canadian and Hawaiian cultures and interests.

Her extensive travel experiences in these countries have provided her work an invaluable asset to her writing.

To all the gang at Newman College of Education, Birmingham
Thank you for the happy memories!

Antonina Irena Brzozowska

FRAGMENTS OF A LIFE

AUSTIN MACAULEY PUBLISHERS™

LONDON * CAMBRIDGE * NEW YORK * SHARJAH

A CIP catalogue record for this title is available from the British Library.

ISBN 9781035869459 (Paperback)
ISBN 9781035869466 (ePub e-book)

www.austinmacauley.com

First Published 2024
Austin Macauley Publishers Ltd®
1 Canada Square
Canary Wharf
London
E14 5AA

To all the team at Austin Macauley Publishers; thank you.

To all who have supported and encouraged me along the way;
thank you.

Sarah

The three loud knocks on the door made her jump; she had not been expecting anyone. Swiftly wiping the remnants of frothy soapy suds from her hands, she hastened to the door.

"Sarah Lisle?" A thinly plucked eyebrow rose in question, the caller's brown eyes directly focused on the puzzled woman standing before her.

"Yes, I am Sarah Lisle." The younger woman's eyes narrowed further, unable to register the identity of the visitor.

"This is for you, Miss Lisle; do with it as you wish." The stranger's words were cold, detached and uncaring as she thrust a brown package into Sarah's hands, turned abruptly and, unheeding her recipient's rapid questions, hastily *click-click-clicked* down the short drive; leaving a bewildered Sarah to tentatively hold on to the mysterious, cumbersome object in her hands, which was shrouded from view in brown crinkly paper; her bemused eyes following the straight-backed, navy-suited woman as she became smaller and smaller, until she turned the corner and vanished out of sight.

Her eyes dropped to the bulky brown package in her hands then, turning abruptly on her heels, she walked back indoors and placed the item onto the kitchen table. Slowly, her fingers unwrapped the brown layer, her eyes becoming wider and growing in incredulity as the layer fell away and more was revealed, making her blood turn ice-cold, her heart freeze over and her disbelieving eyes stare unblinkingly at what she saw before her.

Slowly the cogs of her temporarily paralysed brain began to whirr. This, she told herself, closing her eyes tightly to block the object from view, is a very sick joke, or is it a figment of my imagination? An envelope, attached to the suspicious-looking item, crashed into her line of vision as she opened her unwilling eyes. Roughly snatching the envelope, she covered the intrusive bulk with its crinkly blanket and switched her attention to the sealed envelope in her hand; curiosity and her wild imagination fighting a mighty war in her whirling head, making her guts twist and writhe with inexplicable fear, whilst her frantic brain cells wondered, whether there was anything or *anybody* inside.

For long, dead minutes, she sat rigid, her heart throbbing heavily, mercilessly; her thoughts drifting to the mysterious woman who had brought the urn to her door and wondering what all this was about.

Scrutinising the hand-written address on the envelope, a wave of horror seeped into her soul shrouding her with inexplicable fear. The handwriting was familiar. For long seconds, her eyes lingered on the perfectly formed letters, following the cursive deflection of each ascender and descender then, cautiously as if handling a rare piece of jewellery, she opened the seal, withdrew the note and read, '*Hi Sarah, I bet you thought you'd heard the last of me, eh…?'*

Tremulous fingers dropped the note onto the table, as if it was a piece of burning coal, her heart clamping by an invisible, incandescent, avaricious band, becoming tighter and tighter until she felt her lungs gasping for air. "This is a sick joke, conjured up by a very sick guy," she stated loudly as she stuffed the partly-read note, with the urn, into the very depths of the kitchen cupboard, slamming hard the door on the items, as an array of memories unleashed themselves in her whirling head; memories she had buried deep—deep and had fervently wished never to resurrect; painful memories that were better off dead and buried.

Throughout the long and torturous night, Sarah tossed and turned; lay rigidly, still eyes glaring at the gloomy ceiling above; roamed around the kitchen making umpteen mugs of tea and left each one untouched; stared at the television screen, which displayed endless moving images and saw none; scanned the first page of a best-seller and failed to register a single word, while all the while one single thought invaded and grew in her chaotic mind, making its home there while all around, she felt, her life falling apart. Pulling out a chair, she sat closing her eyes; tighter and tighter she squeezed, trying desperately to obliterate the offending image from her mind and the more she tried it became more prominent, clearer; more stark in its undeniable reality. The image was Peter Brooke, the man who had ruined her life; the man whose ashes rested inside an urn, in her kitchen cupboard under her sink.

Peter Brooke had the pick of women at his disposal, but he always aimed for one type of female, the one who was out of reach; unavailable; a challenge to overcome and conquer, by fair means or foul. Some challenges were easy; others were hard to achieve and some harder still, but *achievement* was the name of the game and Peter Brooke settled for nothing less though, of course, there was always the odd exception to the rule. When he attained what he determinedly strived to achieve, he would quickly tire of his prize, abandon it and aim for the next. It didn't matter whose feelings he hurt in the process; whose heart he trampled on or broke. What mattered was the goal and he was a master in his art.

One evening Sarah had walked into the crowded, buzzing pub; one among many of her factory work colleagues, about to celebrate a friend's hen party. It was the last place on earth Sarah Lisle wished to be seen in, but it was her best friend's night and there had been no get-out clause. Begrudgingly, she followed an excitable Julie, and a hoard of half-cut hens, into the pub, psyching herself up for a long and torturous evening.

He heard them before he saw them, not thinking much of them or their boisterous behaviour; turning his back on them and his full attention on the bevvy of beauties gathered protectively around him, for there was never a short supply where Peter Brooke was concerned; each female thinking herself to be jolly lucky to be anywhere within his ten-metre radius. He focused his green steely eyes back on his long-standing girlfriend, Amy Pilkington, and continued his charm offensive.

The evening wore happily on when suddenly there were loud gasps, cheers and rapturous applause as, making his determined way through the rowdy revellers, a pristinely attired *policeman,* with an uncharacteristic cheeky grin, strode purposefully into the midst of the *hens* to the delightful amusement and squeals of all, but one.

Sarah's eyes widened with the ultimate horror, her heart pounding as an overwhelming surge of embarrassment rushed through her entire body, suffusing her face with a shade of beetroot red. Before the handsome, sexy *policeman* could take off his jacket she was off like the wind, pushing her way through the excited crowd, spilling their assorted drinks, hearing the echo of their expletives thrown at her, as she finally broke out into the cool night air and took a deep breath.

Propped against the wall, her fast-pumping heart struggled to regain its normal rhythm, as her eyes looked out onto the autumnal silhouetted clump of trees in the grounds. Staring unblinkingly at the shadowed skeletal trees, their rugged twisted branches barely visible against the dark backdrop of sky, she asked out loudly, "Why am I like this; why can't I enjoy myself like the rest of them; why do I have to be different?"

"Different is good."

Abruptly, Sarah's body turned ninety degrees anti-clockwise, her wide startled eyes staring at the figure before her, as her mouth opened and closed before it clamped hard on the rude words trying to escape; her bemused eyes dropping to a slither of a smile on a stranger's lips, betraying his inner amusement.

"You know, talking to yourself might be construed as the first sign of lunacy," he smirked devilishly, his green eyes twinkling.

"And listening into another person's private conversation is damned right rude." She hissed, feeling an overwhelming surge of anger towards this stranger for, how dare he—But before she had time to analyse her uncharacteristic fury, her ears were subjected to further analytical scrutiny.

"A conversation with who; as far as I can see, apart from you and I, there is no one else here?"

Snapping her eyes shut in defeat, she felt her blood, burning full of pure animosity towards this obnoxious intruder, surge through her fast-pulsating veins. "It's none of your business," she retorted savagely as she brushed past him, accidentally dislodging his cigarette from his fingers while his eyes, a mixture of amusement and curiosity, watched her scurry back inside.

While she glared disdainfully at the tall, all-but-naked, *policeman* cavorting around, Peter Brooke intently observed Sarah beneath surreptitiously hooded shrewd eyes, knowing for a fact he was going to bump into her again.

The bride looked beautiful in her white satin streamlined dress, as did Sarah complementing her best friend in a figure-hugging, deep purple full gown, with diamanté studs interspersed discreetly into the swirly curls of her bun. And as Julie, her father and her bridesmaids elegantly walked down the aisle, one pair of secretive eyes watched the proceedings with avid interest, his green eyes lingering on one person in particular, his mind focused on one purpose in mind; a new and exciting challenge and one he was looking forward to with relish.

Sarah played her role to perfection. Only she was aware that, if it had not been for her prior visit to the doctor, and the little pills she had consumed before the ceremony, she would not be here at all. The pills were her crutch, which gave her much-needed confidence to face others; to face the world, and at times, to face herself. It was a secret she shared only with her medical practitioner. As far as the outside world was concerned, Sarah Lisle was always brimming with confidence, except on the evening of the hen party, the evening she had run out of her little white pills.

He watched somewhat bemused, for the woman he had heard talking to herself a few days ago, was not the self-assured woman talking to everyone now. She looked different too, he pondered. Then, she had reminded him of a timid mouse; now, she was more of a social butterfly, fluttering from one happy guest to another; laughing, joking and drinking. Yes, she was certainly a mystery; a mystery he wouldn't mind unravelling, he mused, forcing himself to divert his eyes from Sarah and switch them back on to the woman standing next to him, his plus one and girlfriend.

Her heart stopped, her incredulous eyes denying whom she had spotted. It couldn't be *him*, she told herself. What on earth would he be doing here? Abruptly diverting her eyes, she brought a glass up to her lips and swallowed the remaining contents in one go hoping the clear, potent liquid would still her fast-beating heart. Her heart stilled, her curiosity grew; her eyes took a furtive look in the direction she did not want to look, for fear of what she may see. Immediately they told her all she didn't want to know. It was *him*! And, he was looking straight at her. For tensed moments, she sat rigidly her eyes transfixed, her mouth bone-dry, her teeth biting her lower lip, while a surge of undiluted panic grew rapidly in the pit of her gnawing stomach, and surged through every fibre in her body and, she knew, no amount of Doctor Emmerton's pills would suffice to quell her deep foreboding. The urge to run overtook her; to run, she knew not where. She sat glued to the spot, her transfixed, glazed eyes on the man she inexplicably wanted to run away from while he stood, raised his glass to her, gave her a cheeky smile and turned his attention back onto the ever-attentive Amy.

Surrounding her on all sides were jovial guests; drinking, talking, dancing; some laughing raucously, already under the influence of the potent stuff; others involved in serious bouts of conversation, and several more engaged in trivial snippets of gossip, or fragments of conversation about unimportant things, to be forgotten as soon as they moved away. Sarah's eyes switched from a loving couple snatching a not-so-private kiss to a group of guests still eating at the table, to a group of work colleagues sharing a joke, to Peter Brooke who was extending his hand to his girlfriend in an invitation to dance. Amy Pilkington jumped at the chance and, eyes riveted, Sarah watched. What was it about this obnoxious, self-assured, over-confident man that was grabbing her reluctant attention? What was so alluring about this stranger? What was it that made him so fascinating? Whatever it was, she determined, she would have to snap out of it; pronto!

Her eyes remained on him. And, he knew it, for he had seen it happening hundreds of times before. Peter Brooke was well aware of the influence he had on women of all ages, creeds and colours; he knew exactly how to play the field and win the end game.

Surrounded by her friends, Sarah's eyes remained hypnotically fixed on the object of her scorn and, as she watched him dancing with one woman after another, her eyes switched to Amy who was deeply engrossed in conversation with two men, making Sarah wonder what kind of relationship, this strange couple with the roving eyes had; snapping out of her reverie as Julie's new husband, and her old-time friend, asked her to dance.

After the waltz ended, she was dutifully escorted back to her seat but before she had the chance to sit down, she felt a cool, broad hand touch her sleeveless arm, making her startled eyes shoot upwards, feeling a hoard of goose pimples invading her flesh and two green eyes staring down at her. "May I have the pleasure?" He extended both his hands in an exaggerated dance pose and waited for her reply.

Her wide, startled eyes swept past his inviting hands and rose to his resolute chin lingering on his smooth, warm smile; they rose further and rested on his steady eyes, which seemed to see into the depths of her very soul. He swam before her eyes, as did everybody and everything else as the guests, the walls, the laden tables of food and drink, and the chairs all meshed into a blurry blob, and she felt her legs wobble and turn to jelly as her racing heart pumped mercilessly faster and faster.

"Well?"

She heard the faint, distant echo of his voice. "I…erm…no…erm…"

"Come on, Miss Indecisive."

And before she could object further, she found herself being guided onto the dance floor, her insides simultaneously twisting and gnawing in silent rebellion.

One redeemable feature of the whole ghastly scenario was the fact that the dance was not the type to promote intimacy; the rock and roll number was fast and lively, though that did nothing to subdue Sarah's inner agitation. In fact, quite the reverse, the mere touch of his hand on hers sent an array of tiny electric sparks up and down her spine, which swiftly travelled to each nerve ending and set each one on fire, sending her mind in a complete whirl until the dance ended and she felt a wave of blessed relief; her short-lived respite dissipating, when he bent his head to hers and said in a low, sexy drawl, "I shall see you again, Sarah."

Involuntarily, her eyes shot up to his as she watched him retreat, leaving her with a shedload of questions. Who was this strange man; how did he know her name and, more importantly, who told him? That night she tossed and turned, the brief sleep she managed to snatch interspersed with interweaving hazy images of the stranger, his soft voice echoing, *I shall see you again, Sarah.*

Tentative enquiries in the following days revealed the stranger was called Peter Brooke. He was, in fact, an associate of Paul, Julie's new husband, and he was a renowned womaniser. Apparently, she was told, women were drawn to him like moths to a flame but, try as they did, he had never succumbed to the commitment of marriage and was never likely to; he loved his playboy image, and himself, far too much to give himself wholly to anyone else. Keep well clear of this Casanova; he is a no-go area, Julie had warned her. But, annoyingly, the more Sarah found out about the mysterious Peter Brooke, the more she wanted to know about him. He was an enigma and she loved puzzles even if, sometimes, they proved to be futile. And so, she pursued her quest for information and found out that this Peter Brooke character had an open relationship with his on-off girlfriend, and he always got any woman he happened to fancy. "Well, not me," she stated loudly, and now knowing everything she possibly wanted to know about him, and believing she would never again see him in this world, she pushed him to the back of her mind fervently hoping that, in time, he would evaporate from her thoughts completely.

She started seeing Brian, a colleague in the packing department of a lingerie factory, where they both worked. She had always got on well with Brian; a reliable, honest, kind, popular chap, who got on well with everyone and would never dream of hurting a fly, let alone a woman he was dating. Their friendship blossomed and soon they became an item and Peter Brooke vanished into the mists of time.

Within weeks, Brian had proposed to Sarah and she had accepted his hand in marriage, and though it seemed to others somewhat of a whirlwind romance, they were both firm in their convictions. They married, and a year to the day, Sarah gave birth to their son.

Peter Brooke had placed Sarah on the back burner but had not forgotten her. He had heard that she'd got married and had a son. These inconveniences, in his point of view, were merely a fly in the ointment and could easily be scraped away. He had a long-term goal and knew, without a doubt, that he would achieve it.

Seven Years Later

Everything in Sarah's life seemed to have turned out perfectly. She and Brian worked hard, and through the fruits of their labour, they had bought a semi-detached house, built an extension, and were hoping for an addition to the family, a playmate for their son, Toby. Getting pregnant a second time, however, was proving to be something of an elusive dream and, after trying to conceive for two years without any sign of success, they mutually decided to seek medical help.

She ran out of the large, sprawling building, her breathing ragged, her throat bone-dry, an overwhelming surge of nervous tension invading every sinew, and rushing through every fast-pulsating vein in her slender frame; the fierce knot in her tightly clenched stomach becoming tighter by the second; the words reverberating in her ears, the last words she had been expecting or wanting to register. Her feet turned a sharp left, her head buzzing whilst still urging her feet to move faster—faster; she had to get out—breathe. The collision brought her to a sudden stop; her shocked eyes eyeballing a stranger, who seemed familiar in an inexplicable way.

"Sorry," he mumbled, placing a determined foot forward to make a hasty retreat. "Sarah?"

Stark eyes returned to the stranger where they locked with his eyes and, in the brief silent seconds which followed, she knew, she had seen this man before; but where? Frantically, she searched her racing brain and couldn't, for the life of her, come up with an answer.

His words crashed into her whirling thoughts. "It's Peter; Peter Brooke." Immediately, his eyes registered her bemused look. "I am the guy who found you kind of talking to yourself; the guy who danced with you at…"

Dredged from the mists of time, it was slowly coming back to her—the guy who had haunted her mind all those years ago; the womaniser; the one she was warned to avoid at all costs; the guy she was now unblinkingly staring at; the guy who was making her heart thump. The years had certainly taken their toll on him, she assessed silently. They had not been kind to him at all. The self-assured man looked old and haggard; his twinkling green eyes had lost their shine and were eclipsed by pain. "Are you all right?" She caught herself asking, and instantly admonished herself severely for her spontaneous words; placing one impatient foot in front of the other, urging to get away from him and into the safety of her car.

"Yes…no…no…"

"Now; what's the answer, Mister Indecisive?" She couldn't control the escaping chuckle, as flashes of a similar conversation gate-crashed her mind.

A stifled nervous laugh escaped his lips, saying nothing but silently telling her everything. He was not all right; a blind person could see he was far from being all right, but she quickly told herself that Peter Brooke was not her problem. She had a far greater problem to tackle. She proceeded to advance forward.

"No; stop. Please, don't go, Sarah."

Her itchy feet remained still on the terra firma; his raw, urgent plea reaching her heart. "Are you all right?" She asked a second time waiting for some kind of reassurance, which would give her the green light to abandon him without fear of guilt.

"No, I am not." The stark words were not ones she wanted to hear.

"Will you have a coffee with me please, Sarah?"

She turned to face him, pinned on her best smile, silently nodded her head, and immediately regretted her decision.

Sitting opposite him in a busy hospital cafeteria, her eyes dropped to his skinny hand, as he poured out the steaming coffee into two cups; shocked to see the protruding blue veins, her eyes rising to his drawn, thin face; but, it was his eyes which told her everything. How sad, pained, hopeless, desolate and, above all, lonely they looked, she surmised.

"I am dying, Sarah." He cut into her bleak assessment of him, her eyes lingering on his as she stared into the abyss of despair. "I am dying," he repeated in case she hadn't heard him. "I have ten months; maybe a year at the very most."

Without warning, an overwhelming tsunami of hot, bubbling anger crashed through every fast-pulsating vein in her body, threatening to explode with devastating consequences, as she stared wide-eyed at the skeletal man before her; the man who had the sheer audacity to lay his dismal fate at her door; a troubled, lonely dying man, who had turned to someone he barely knew for a grain of comfort. Involuntarily, she extended her hand and clasped his lean hand, feeling the jutting bones, making her instantly flinch inwardly. Forcing her lips into a warm smile, she wrenched the words out of her dry mouth, "I am listening, Peter."

Within half an hour, her head was buzzing mercilessly, her feet itching to get away; yet, she remained on her chair and listened; two untouched cold coffees on the table.

"Please can I see you again, Sarah?"

She felt his appealing eyes on her and nodded. "Half past two; Tuesday afternoon; same place."

Her heart as heavy as stone, she walked in through the front door, knowing that what she had to tell her husband would be more than he could stomach.

He stared at her his eyes wide, aghast and disbelieving. She knew it would be like this, but she had to tell him, if they had any hope of moving on with their lives and so she persevered, knowing she would have to deceive the man she loved more than life itself.

Taking both her hands in his warm hands, he gazed intently into her still eyes, but she could only feel the parchment-like skin and jutting bones of Peter's hands, as her husband's gentle words sent icy shivers through her body. "We will do everything we need to do, Sarah. I shall support you all the way if you want to go through the ordeal."

Her head nodded vigorously. "Yes, I am ready, Brian," she stated hoping her words sounded steady and believable; her eyes stubbornly riveted to their clasped hands for fear of betraying herself; for, it was Brian who failed to function in the conceiving stage of proceedings; it was Brian who was firing blanks.

That night they made love and while he caressed, thrust, sighed and pronounced his undying love; she faked it all.

Placing one foot in front of the other trepidation, like a heavy boulder, weighed her down. Briefly, she glanced backwards whilst continuing to walk forwards. Now was the chance to change her mind; to run back to her loving, trusting husband and the security of her home and family. Instead, she turned, accelerated her pace and prepared to encounter her fate.

She espied him from afar, her pounding heart skipping a beat. Her eyes lingered on the lone figure, a cup tightly clasped in both hands, blank eyes staring into oblivion; or was he, she thought, staring at his own mortality? Cautiously she placed one foot in front of the other and proceeded to walk towards the huddled figure, forcing a smile. "Hello, Peter," she said softly, making him abruptly swing around, drops of black coffee spilling onto his skinny hands; a veil of relief spreading visibly over his drawn, anxious face.

"I didn't think you'd come."

"Seemingly, you don't know me at all."

"Seemingly, I don't," he agreed, "I'll get you a coffee."

She watched as his skeletal frame walked towards the counter. What the hell am I doing here? She scolded herself severely. Where are his hordes of women; where are all his adoring fans? Where is Amy Pilkington? Her questions roamed about her head unanswered as Peter approached with two fresh, steaming drinks.

For long, silent seconds they sat, shrouded by a prickly blanket of unease, while people came and went; the odd patient clad in pyjamas, accompanied by a loved one, relieved to get out of the ward and cafeteria staff clearing up tables. Sarah raised her eyes to the broken man sitting in front of her and said what was fermenting in her mind. "What happened to Amy?"

The coarse, bitter laugh emitted from his dry mouth made her brow furrow, his words penetrating her conscience. "She'd finally had enough, that's what happened. Like all the others she wanted a husband, a home and kids. She got them all. She is now happily married and expecting her third."

A lump rose to Sarah's throat. She swallowed hard. This, she told herself firmly, was no time to wallow in her own misfortunes. "I am sorry," she managed to squeeze the three words out of her dry mouth.

"I'm not," he hissed.

But clearly, she could tell by the raw hate in his tone, he was.

"So you see, my dear, Sarah, I am left completely on my own in my hour of need, with someone I barely know to hold my hand, so to speak."

"Better someone you barely know than no one at all; besides, you may be able to help me, Peter." The second the last word flew out of her mouth, she knew there was no going back.

"How?" His brows shot up.

His one solitary word cut sharply through her conscience, with the force of a recently sharpened blade through the ice; slicing mercilessly through her values, morals, responsibilities and loyalty and lacerating them ruthlessly into tiny jagged fragments, where nothing made sense anymore and all was permissible. "I can give you comfort in your darkest hours; you, in return, can give me a baby." Her clear, concise words cut through her heart, for in the seconds of spewing them out, she was firmly ensconced in the act of betraying her husband; the only man she ever truly loved. The seed of deceit was sown.

"What?" He gasped spluttering, spilling his coffee. And, while he struggled to compose himself, she repeated her statement calmly, coolly and collectively.

Laborious minutes ticked by. Sarah and Peter stared into their cups, their minds furiously whirling.

"Ok, I'll do it." His detached, cold words hit her with an almighty force, stirring her guts into a fierce, frenzied state of writhing and gnawing, as her heart soared to the highest heavens and plummeted back down to the depths of hell; covering her flesh with excited goose pimples; making her eyes sparkle and almost simultaneously dull; causing her happy state of euphoria to violently crash down around her, while she asked herself over and over again, What have I done; what can of worms have I opened up?

Hours later, she lay rigid beside her sleeping husband, her eyes staring unblinkingly at the dark ceiling, her own thoughts haunting her heart and soul. When she finally managed to snatch snippets of sleep, it was interspersed with nightmarish fragments of blurred images as Brian and Peter mingled and intermingled, weaved and interweaved; their mouths, like shadowy caverns, gruesomely opening wide and thrusting forth poisonous venom and untold revenge, as they yelled and screamed and—yelled louder and more ferociously until she jumped with a start. Surreptitiously glancing to her side, she noticed Brian was still in the phase of soundless sleep, the duvet lightly rising and falling in rhythm with his breathing.

Throwing the bed cover to one side, she rose, haphazardly threw on her velvet housecoat and strode down to the eerily still kitchen. Pouring a glass of water she ascended the stairs, slowly opened Toby's door and stepped inside his room, switching on the bedside light. Perching on a stool her eyes carefully took everything in, as if seeing the interior of her son's room for the first time, a smile sliding onto her lips as her eyes scanned the wallpaper; Spiderman was the boy's ultimate hero and woe betide anyone speaking a word against him. Her eyes flitted randomly across rows upon rows of books on the homemade bookshelves, ranging from Robinson Crusoe to Huckleberry Finn and a series of non-fiction books too. She spotted one about Florence Nightingale; another about King Henry the Eighth. Her eyes left the rows of books and darted to a corner of the room, where an assortment of sporting gear had been dumped: football boots and ball, cricket bat, swimming goggles; a damp towel that should have been placed in the laundry basket. Her eyes rested on her sleeping son, the echo of his words coming vividly to mind… *I'd love a brother or a sister, Dad…*as he and Brian planted seeds in the garden. She was the surreptitious eavesdropper, who had heard the words through an open kitchen window whilst washing pots. An innocent request, she now told herself, but wasn't it what she and Brian wanted? Peter Brooke crashed into her mind and, as she closed the door on her sleeping son, her mind was made up, and this time there was no going back.

They met under the cover of darkness, in a small motel, fifteen kilometres away from town. As far as Brian and Toby were concerned, Sarah was staying over with one of her friends, who was feeling under the weather; they had no cause to doubt her.

They had sex; raw sex, leaving Sarah with the heavy weight of deceit running through every vein in her body; a new hope beating in her heart and the bleak thought of payback to come, for come it surely would.

She continued on her journey of betrayal and deceit. Brian had succumbed to her wish of attending consultations on her own; her treatment had started, as far as he was concerned, and now they were both waiting for the whole thing to come to fruition and, finally, they were rewarded. Sarah was pregnant and the family revelled in their joy, though one member's heart was heavily suffused with the burden of a lie.

Peter was duly informed of her pregnancy and kept his promise of keeping well out of it. Her promise was still to be fulfilled and she knew the time was fast approaching.

On a bright and sunny late spring morning, the phone rang shrilly, thrusting Sarah out of a dark reverie. "Hello," she snapped.

"Hello… Sarah… Is that you, Sarah?"

Her heart turned to ice.

The voice on the other end of the line sounded faint, distant and somehow detached, but she identified the caller immediately. "Yes…yes, it's me." She peered around the door but, to her relief, could neither see nor hear either Brian or Toby.

"I need you… Sarah."

Her iced heart sprang to life and thudded mercilessly. This was the time she needed to fulfil her part of the bargain; her promise to a dying man. This was the time to show her true grit. If only she had a packet of Doctor Emmerton's white pills. She heard the *click* of the outside door and the sound of approaching footsteps. "I'll be there," she rushed the words out and placed the receiver back onto its cradle, but not before she heard Peter's voice. "Thank you; thank you so very much, Sarah." His grateful voice grated in her head; they were words that would haunt her for the rest of her life.

Again, Sarah's friend was under the weather, or so Brian was told and accepted Sarah's words readily without a flicker of suspicion; waving to his wife as she took a fleeting glance backwards before she stepped into the car; her deceitful heart heavy with remorse, as she switched on the ignition and brought the motor into life, her free hand resting on her small bump; the reason of her betrayal. The engine purred; the car stood motionless, her eyes shot to the rear mirror, where she saw Brian and Toby waving her off, making her deceitful heart turn to stone.

Sitting perfectly still, like a solidified statue, she espied her husband and son running towards her. Swiftly releasing the hand brake and slamming hard, the accelerator pedal, she fled the scene.

She had never been to Peter Brooke's residence but had heard it was well out of town, twenty-three kilometres away in fact, and she had also heard that he lived in sumptuous surroundings, envied by many. Twenty-three kilometres, she told herself, was enough distance to compose herself; to prepare mentally for whatever she was to encounter and she knew, without a doubt, it was not going to be good.

Each kilometre was overwhelmingly laborious; each kilometre seeming like ten; each kilometre bringing her nearer and nearer to the place of doom and impending death. Her fingers stretched to the dial of the radio and stopped at the sound of a happy, carefree tune playing heavily in her ears. She turned the radio off and stared starkly ahead and, instead of the winding country road, she saw a cheerful Brian and happy Toby waving her off—a dying man gasping for his last breath—a dying man; his image superseded the previous happy image and hung heavily in her mind and grew and grew, larger and larger and more grotesque in its clarity and reality, until she could see nothing and no one but Peter Brooke's deathly-white, drawn face; his sunken eyes staring unblinkingly at the only person he could rely on. Slamming hard on the brake pedal she forced the car into an emergency stop, propelling her whole body to thrust forward and a big, white cushion to blow up in her face. For long, silent minutes she sat, her head encased in the depths of the white substance, her thoughts dead.

The loud screeching of a horn jerked her out of oblivion. Bewildered, wide eyes gazed cautiously around as she came to the conclusion that she was on a country road; a figure from a nearby abandoned car hastily approaching her vehicle, whilst her chaotic mind whirled and whirred, unable to formulate one coherent thought. In the frantic minutes that followed, an ambulance and a couple of policemen were on the scene, a breathalyser was administered, and seconds later, she was whisked away. She made only one urgent phone call to the man that mattered.

He came to collect her; a relieved man, who could not see his future days without this woman he relied on. "Oh love." He fell into her open arms and his arms enfolded her, while she felt only the rawness of betrayal for the man she had deceived; a dying man, who would now have to leave this world with no one by his side.

On a bleak October morning, the sound of a baby's cry filled the small room, making two hearts soar to the highest heaven, and one heart to plummet to the depths of hell.

Brian picked up the ominous envelope addressed to him and scrutinised carefully the handwriting, his brow furrowing at the unrecognisable text. Roughly tearing the envelope open, he sat down and read the contents, his heart rapidly turning to ice.

"Are you ok, Brian?" She smiled warmly as the sound of the baby's cry made her hasten to its source, and Brian's guts to gnaw and twist mercilessly, his entire world crashing in and around him. Closing his eyes, he squeezed them tightly, against the excruciating sound of his wife's soothing voice, mingled with the infant's cry.

The slamming of the door made Sarah jump. After a second, she continued to rock the baby; the source of her betrayal and the only living soul she had left in the world.

Brian never walked back into the family home and neither did Toby, for the woman they both loved had destroyed both their worlds.

Present Time

The chimes of the clock barged into Sarah's private thoughts; rising abruptly she headed towards the kitchen unit, withdrew a piece of paper and silently read the words.

'Hi Sarah,

I bet you thought you'd heard the last of me, eh?

I'll come straight to the point. You are the most evil, self-centred woman it was ever my misfortune to have known, and I have known many women in my time.

You not only betrayed your husband, your son, yourself and me; you betrayed our daughter, and yes, I know you had a daughter, for your husband kindly informed me. Being the upstanding man he has always been, he thought I had a right to know.

I have given you a part of myself, to remind you of your broken promise; a promise to a dying man, who had hoped for a grain of comfort in his darkest hour.

Do with me what you will; quite frankly, my dear, I have gone past caring. However, our daughter will also have a part of me, to be given to her in a specially made locket on her thirteenth birthday. Your husband has assured me he will not break his promise.

So farewell, Sarah. Let our daughter be an everlasting reminder to you of your betrayal and deceit.

Peter'

A solitary tear fell and created an immediate smudge on the paper obscuring his name, but his image was firmly secured in her head and that, she knew, would never be obliterated, no matter how hard she tried to erase him from her memory for, lest she forget, their daughter would be there to remind her. Plunging her hand back into the cupboard, she withdrew the bulky brown package, her heart racing wildly. Fingers trembling, she unwrapped the paper and withdrew the shiny urn, placing it carefully onto the table; her eyes drawn to the folded paper taped to the urn. Peeling it away she unfolded the paper and read aloud, 'Memorial Service of the late, Peter Brooke. Saint Sebastian's church. 10 November at 10.30 a.m.' Placing the note, together with the urn and Peter's note, back into the bowels of the cupboard, she closed the unit door firmly.

Emma

"Catch me if you can, Gary!" The skimpily attired blonde ran behind the plush cream sofa and crouched there in eager anticipation; her large, expectant, blue eyes darting this way and that, her ears attuned to every sound, but the sound of stealthily approaching bare feet from behind.

"Gotcha!"

She felt his large, broad hands around her tiny waist, as he turned her around and lowered his lips onto her lips, swiftly withdrew them, picked her up and threw her onto the sofa. Ripping off her T-shirt, his expert fingers deftly unclasped her bra; his handsome, rugged face looming over her when—they froze. The shrill ring of the doorbell penetrated the silence. "Ignore it," Gary urged, his lips smothering her lips, cheeks and throat with hot kisses; his cock on fire. The second impatient ring propelled Emma into successfully wriggling her way out of her boyfriend's possessive clutches and to the door. She raised her finely plucked eyebrows. "Yes?"

"Emma Brown?"

"Yes."

"For you."

Emma's puzzled eyes dropped down to the curious-looking package, in the woman's black leather-gloved hands. "Are you sure; I'm not expecting anything?"

"I'm sure," snapped the middle-aged woman, and before Emma could contest further, the stranger was disappearing down the drive the *click-click-click* of her stilettos reverberating in Emma's ears.

As she closed the door she heard Gary's impatient voice, "Come on, Em; what's keeping you?"

"Agh!"

The thud on the carpet brought Gary to the hallway, where he encountered a wide-eyed, pale-faced Emma, and as he lowered his puzzled eyes, he looked at something which looked like an urn and around the opened top a sprinkling of grainy, grey ashes. A furrow appearing on his forehead, he tried to figure out

26

what all this was about, his ears succumbed to the sound of a second thud; his eyes darting to a sprawled-out girlfriend, beside an urn and its sprinkled contents.

"Oh my God," he mumbled scratching his head, adding incoherently, "Surely it can't be… Fluffball," as images of Emma's beloved sheepdog, and the bitter account of the war of custody Emma fought with her ex and lost, crashed into his mind. His eyes drifted to the ashes. "Oh, I am sorry, mate." He mumbled, hastily shovelling the ashes up with his hands and dropping them back into the urn, before turning to his girlfriend, who was now showing some signs of life. "Em-Emma—are you all right?"

She blinked once, twice, her eyes rising to the urn, which was now resting on a side table. "Get it away from me! Get it away from me!" She shrieked repeatedly and uncontrollably, like a demented parrot.

Immediately, he obeyed her request and deposited the receptacle onto the kitchen table, returned and cradled Emma's trembling body in his strong arms. "Is it *him*, Em?" He cautiously asked in the softest voice he could muster.

Is it him? His words reverberated in her swimming head, a sudden icy realisation hitting her like a thunderbolt immediately creating a fresh, more vigorous, bout of trembling. "It can't be… It can't be…" She slowly shook her head from side to side.

"Sh…" Gary rocked her gently in his arms, wondering how on earth he could smooth this matter over, before getting her back in the sack, not that that got him anywhere either, for he was fast learning that his girlfriend was an expert flirt, but when it came down to business, it was another matter entirely. But, he liked her; he liked her a lot and there was always—hope.

"Could it be *him*, Gary?" She asked her words barely audible.

And before Gary could deny all such *foolish* notions, she'd unravelled herself from his arms and hastened towards the kitchen, where she stopped rigid before the urn as thoughts came flooding back.

For long torturous minutes, she stood silently and stared and, for long torturous minutes, Gary stood silently beside her. Finally, her fingers reached forward and gingerly they pulled away the layer of brown paper, which Gary had thoughtfully replaced minutes earlier; her eyes dropping to a folded piece of paper. She picked it up, her eyes dropping to the signature and read aloud in a faltering voice, 'From Peter.' She felt her legs wobble and buckle beneath her; saw the walls, chairs, table, oven and everything else merge together in a blur and go round and round and, once again, felt Gary's strong arms scoop her up.

"How-how could he, Gary? How could that despicable man just despatch my beloved Fluffball in this way, without any prior warning?" She sobbed bitterly; her heart, mind, body and soul ripping with uncontrollable grief, while Gary's lips remained firmly clamped, deciding no amount of words would explain Brooke's atrocious behaviour.

There was no lovemaking that night; not that there was any most nights. Still, he thought to himself, he must be strong for Emma, and by fighting her corner, he could score some points in his favour.

Throughout the long night, Emma tossed, turned and finally threw the duvet to Gary's side, wrapped her luxurious robe around her slender body, withdrew the urn from its resting place and sat staring at the glossy pot which, she mused, contained her beloved pet and the memories came flooding back… He had been a Christmas present from Peter; the best Christmas present she had ever had and the most cherished. From the moment she saw the little, white and black fluffy puppy she fell madly in love with it; in fact, she grew to love him far more than she loved the benefactor; this, in turn, created a heavy streak of resentment in Peter Brooke's heart, causing him to wish he had never bought her the puppy in the first place. And so, the battle for Emma's love commenced and the puppy won every single time… Emma's lips formed into a whimsical smile, her fingers lightly caressing the smooth silkiness of the mahogany urn.

"There was no contest really was there, Fluffball?" She said aloud and in her mind, she could hear him bark back his affirmative answer. Her mind drifted back to the evening…she literally bumped into Peter, as they were both buying drinks at a crowded bar; both unashamedly flirting with others whilst, now and again, throwing the obligatory reassuring glances to their respective partners… I should have heeded the warning signs, she told herself, for they were there; I just chose to ignore them, she remembered vividly.

Peter Brooke also chose to ignore the warning bells. He and Emma had been formed out of the same mould: good-looking, self-assured, brimming with confidence and both pathological flirts; both hurt others rather than being hurt themselves and both frequently abandoned their long-suffering partners for a brief, exciting fling with someone else. Only this time, she dismally concluded, one got burnt by a lover's flame. Her mind drifted once more…

Seven Years Earlier

Her eyes flitted across the sea of rowdy revellers and abruptly stopped roving and lingered. He's certainly a looker, she mused, her eyes briefly flicking to the barmaid who was in no hurry to serve her. Her large inquisitive eyes darted back to the stranger and keenly took in his lean, handsome face; his firm jaw; his mouth slightly quivering, as if he was trying to suppress a smile. Her eyes rose to his warm eyes and his dark, curly hair giving him a somewhat boyish look. Definitely a popular guy, she assessed, judging from the horde of females surrounding him and hanging on to his every word. And most definitely an unhinged flirt, she chuckled to herself, as she witnessed him winking mischievously at a stunning redhead and then, seconds later, at a rather plain-looking girl. Emma's curious eyes drank him in until he caught her eye and she abruptly looked away. Why? She did not know why. She was not in the habit of looking away from good-looking men; neither did she shrink away from their attention.

Grabbing a full tray of assorted drinks, she attempted to withdraw from the crowded bar only to be pushed and shoved; her ears subjected to a range of expletives and stubborn bodies who refused to budge a centimetre.

"Here, let me help."

The silky, smooth voice did not register in her brain, but her eyes instantly recognised the guy behind the voice, as her large blue eyes clashed with green twinkling eyes which both hypnotised and repelled her in equal measures. "I can manage, thank you." She snapped, tearing her eyes away and scanning the heaving room for her boyfriend and their mutual crowd of mates.

"I know you can manage but, nevertheless, let me help you, especially as you have already lost half of your drinks."

Her eyes dropped to the pool of liquid on the tray. "Here," she retorted handing him the tray while inwardly a wave of undiluted, inexplicable fury surged through her veins. Was it for this interfering flirt, or for the loss of alcohol? She did not know.

"I thought I'd lost you forever in that crowd," stated Rick her latest beau. "Who's your new friend?"

She whipped back her head, her heart skipping a beat as their eyes clashed once more. "I don't know," she mumbled, "what's your name?"

"Peter. Peter Brooke."

Turning back, she bestowed her full attention on Rick, knowing she had caught another admirer in the net.

"Come on, join us, Pete," enthused Rick. Peter glanced back at his admiring fans and, before he could object, Rick added, "Bring your crowd over too; the more, the merrier, as they say." And, within minutes, they were one big jovial mass, where new friendships were quickly formed and the subtle seeds of betrayal were surreptitiously planted.

Eyes secretly flitted and lingered on eyes, which were already claimed by others. Still, they looked and the more they looked, the more they wanted a taste of the forbidden fruit, and it was always the attraction of the forbidden fruit which made Emma and Peter thrive.

The note Peter managed to secrete into Emma's hand cemented a new beginning, and within a week, Emma and Peter's current flames were out of the picture, at least for the time being and a new flame was lit, though from the very start, it flickered precariously.

Christmas was fast approaching and with it the onset of the party season; a time when often relationships are put to the test, in more ways than one; a time when flirts have boundless opportunities to flourish in their art; a time when hearts are broken…

Peter Brooke's appreciative eyes admired her through the full-length mirror, as they absorbed her skimpy, midnight-blue, sequined dress which finished well above her knees; her slender body and the outline of her pert breasts, secured within a low-cut neckline which complemented her long, slender neck; his hungry eyes resting on her luscious red-lipsticked lips, his breath catching in his throat as his lips curled into a secret smile. Before the night is out, I shall have you, he vowed silently; his smile dying an instant death, as previous failed attempts flashed through his mind, for Emma Brown had proved to be a very tough nut to crack; tough, but not impossible. His smile reappeared.

From the very start, Peter could not fathom this woman out. On the outside, she appeared to be a woman after his own heart; great-looking, confident, a flirt and, above all, a challenge worth pursuing. On the inside, an enigma; a mystery he could not work out and the more he tried, the more confusing she became.

He had successfully lured her away from her current relationship; that was the easy part. Getting to know her a bit was the tricky part. The only thing he was absolutely certain of was that Emma Brown was a massive flirt but, he asked himself, wasn't that part of the whole attraction? He closed his eyes and squeezed them tightly, obliterating her sexy reflection. If only she reined it in a bit; if only she didn't appear to be so readily accessible to all and sundry; if only she wasn't just a tease for, he concluded, to get into her pants was like breaking into Fort Knox; impossible. Still, he mused, his lips breaking into a smile, he had the perfect Christmas present to lure her into temptation.

The bar was smoky and bursting at the seams when they sauntered in and Peter's eyes immediately darted across the available talent waiting for him, the gorgeous hunk, to take his pick. His admiring eyes flitted from blonde to redhead to brunette; from a skinny model to one more generously endowed, before finally resting on the woman standing next to him, whose eyes were also roving. Briefly, their eyes locked, a heavy blanket of entrapment covering them both, suffocating and imprisoning them simultaneously; clipping their wings so that they could not fly and soar. Exchanging forced smiles, they looked away longingly at the flirty couples around them. But, one flirting butterfly was happy to, temporarily, have its wings clipped; to settle on one flower, to suck its nectar and revel in its sweetness.

He scrutinised her every move, as she was led away from him by one of her work colleagues and, though the small dancing area was packed with gyrating bodies, he saw only Emma, felt her every move and heard her flirty laugh as he ached for her touch; his eyes yearning to drown in the depths of her blue pools; his ears burning to hear her intimate innuendoes, which were never intended for him—always for another—never for him—always for another. His jealous blood surged furiously through each throbbing vein—surging…surging—forcing his involuntary feet to move one in front of the other, step by solitary step; one polished shoe stepping onto the dance floor, followed by the other and then both stopped directly in front of the gyrating couple; so lost in the moments of the dance and their flirtations, they were not aware of their intruder, whose burning blood had reached fever point and was threatening to boil over and cover them with its scorching resentment, his jealous eyes throwing invisible daggers at the oblivious couple, while the loud pounding so-called music bombarded his ears; his nose registering the nauseous smell of a nearby sweaty body and the painful sight of *his* woman openly flirting with her dancing partner; his arms around her slender waist bringing her in closer—closer—"Emma."

Closer and closer, she snuggled up to him, until he was almost on top of her as they laughed and gyrated; gyrated and laughed.

"Emma."

The distant echo of her name drifted in and out of her happy head, like a floating feather.

"Emma!"

They continued to laugh and gyrate, totally preoccupied with each other to notice anyone else until—

Eyes dropped to the crumpled bundle on the floor. Nimble feet became motionless. Eyes shot up to a raised clenched fist and a dark, thunderous face. Time stood still. The music pounded relentlessly on. One set of eyes glared; the other stared at the source of his desire as her large blue eyes unblinkingly stared at the source of her scorn. "How could you, Pete?" She finally managed to utter between clenched teeth.

"I could because you're mine, Emma," Peter stated firmly, but just after the last three words were spewed venomously out of his mouth, he desperately wished he could claw them back, as his eyes locked with her unforgiving eyes.

"I belong to no one," she snapped. "Do you hear me, Peter, no one!"

Despite the kaleidoscope of multi-coloured lights splaying sporadically around the small dancing area, obscuring a clear vision of anyone in particular, Peter was sure all had witnessed the surging heat colouring his face; he was in no doubt that every reveller had laughed, and were still laughing, at his trembling body and tightly clenched fists, pitying the poor fellow he had felled; the man called Simon, his rival and foe.

The rest of the evening was a prelude to the days that followed; days filled with mistrust, regret and a desperate, impossible yearning to turn back the clock. The heavy tension-filled atmosphere was in complete contrast to the happy Christmassy feel-good factor outside. Avoidance was the name of the game; at least it was as far as Emma was concerned. She ignored his tentative smiles, his casual enquiries about her day, the mere brush of his fingers against her hand, his sincere attempts at an apology and he knew, without a doubt, that if he volunteered to move out, she would personally pack his suitcase and hold the door wide open.

Rummaging in the depths of a drawer, his fingers found what he was looking for, withdrew the small black velvet box and opened the lid, his eyes gazing on the glittering diamond, surrounded by an array of sapphires; the most expensive ring in the shop. He snapped the lid shut and stuffed the small box deep—deep into his trouser pocket and vacated the house.

She had seen it; the sparkling ring in its small, black, velvet-lined box. An engagement ring, she smiled; her smile dying instantly as images of the green-eyed monster crashed into her head. But, still, an engagement ring!

Something far more precious lay in wait for Emma; a last-ditched attempt at repairing their relationship before the gaping seam was so wide it could never be repaired. He cast a look at his new purchase and smiled. Who could resist? His smile widened.

Christmas Eve arrived and with it came fresh hope. The unfortunate, but not forgotten, incident on the dance floor was avoided at all costs; neither wanted to start yet another argument and neither wanted to be alone at Christmas.

Emma stood at the sink watching the dirty, soapy water gurgle around the plughole until the soapy water, disappeared out of sight; jumping as she felt his arms wrap around her waist and the warm, comforting closeness of his firm body next to hers. She took in a deep breath and sighed deeply, for she had missed his attention. Closing her eyes, she inhaled the musky smell of his aftershave. If only he would say, *sorry*. It was, she knew, never to be; Peter Brooke was not a man of apologies. But, still—She turned and his mouth was immediately upon hers possessive and passionate, his expert tongue invading and probing her mouth, making her body feel as if it was about to explode as she abandoned herself to him.

Lifting her in his strong arms, he carried her up the stairs and into the bedroom. Too late, he realised what he'd done. Still, his racing mind told him, it might be ok as his lips feverishly kissed her cheeks, her mouth, her neck while his impatient fingers frantically unfastened the stubborn buttons on her blouse, finding the clasp of her bra as she grabbled with his fly.

"What was that?"

His ears were deaf to her enquiry as his mouth claimed a nipple.

"Stop!"

He stopped; then continued in his endeavour to claim his prize.

"Stop, Peter, stop!"

Shit, he silently cursed as he begrudgingly obeyed her command, his ears finely attuned to the sound coming from behind the heavy, velvet drape. Shit! Shit! Shit! He cursed, trying desperately to obliterate the infuriating disturbance, as he prepared himself for the delight she was about to savour.

"What was that?" Emma gasped, grabbing her blouse and draping it haphazardly over her naked breasts.

"What?" He asked innocently feigning ignorance whilst, at the same time, damning himself over and over again for his stupid idea, which had so obviously backfired.

"Whimpering; I heard whimpering, Pete." She stared wide-eyed at the half-dressed guy now standing in front of her. "I heard whimpering; a-a dog." Her eyes were wide and expectant as if the creature was about to leap out and sit on its hind legs before her.

He closed his eyes tight. It's just my fucking luck, he execrated repeatedly, but no matter how much he silently and severely admonished himself, his woman was now on a mission and it did not involve his sexual prowess.

"I heard it; I know I heard whimpering, Pete." She turned and stared unblinkingly at nothing in particular. "Ah—there; I heard it—there it is again." Straining her ears, her eyes darted this way and that and finally rested on the drawn curtains. Her feet followed suit, as did Peter's feet, his eager hands about to reclaim the prize he was determined to have. Instead, he claimed two handfuls of air, as she pushed one curtain aside, bent down and retrieved the mystery.

The second she turned towards him, her eyes sparkling and her cheeks glowing, he knew he had lost her. He had, at that precise moment in time, been replaced. The Christmas present he had bought his girlfriend became his cursed nemesis.

His eyes glared, his blood seethed as Emma cooed over, cuddled and pampered Fluffball and, it was only when he saw them cuddled up together on the sofa, he realised a flirt like Emma did not need another flirt in her life. And why, he asked himself, would I need another flirt? His mind drifted back to the enchanting blonde beauty in the bar, his contemptuous eyes glaring at the puppy, as he stated silently, She can have Fluffball; I'm off!

The loud bang of the door reverberated in her ears. Her free hand grabbed the remote and snuggling up closer to her new furry friend, she whispered in Fluffball's ear, "Thank God, he's gone."

Present Time

And now, after all these years, Fluffball was here. Right in front of her, or to be precise, inside the shiny brown urn facing her; dead.

Sinking to the floor, she sobbed raw, salty, heart-wrenching tears; unable to restrain her heartache from showing whilst, involuntarily, she yielded to an overwhelming emotion invading every fibre of her trembling body, making it heave uncontrollably; unaware that her latest beau, Gary, had slid behind her; unconscious of his protective arms around her, feeling only her raw pain lacerating through her, threatening to shred her into a million heart-breaking pieces.

Long minutes passed until finally, her intense sobbing subsided into soft crying, her glassy eyes acquiring a sheen of undiluted anger. How could he? She asked herself over and over again, knowing full well that Peter Brooke could, and Peter Brooke would do anything to gain the upper hand and to have his sweet revenge. But this—this—Her eyes darted back to the shiny urn resting on the table and lowered on the carpet, where she espied a few grainy bits, which had escaped Gary's spontaneous cleaning and her sobbing renewed, accelerating in seconds. She heard the echo of his words and chose to ignore them, wishing he and his stupid words would disappear into oblivion and leave her to grieve her Fluffball in peace.

"Are you sure there isn't a note in that paper bag, Em?" Gary cut into her private world.

The sobs gathered momentum.

"Em?" His eyes darted to his sobbing girlfriend, now slumped against the wall, her knees brought up to and tucked under her chin, on which she rested her grief-beleaguered head. "Em?"

Her sobs grew more intense as her trembling fingers extended to the grains. Gathering them up as if they were rare and precious jewels, she clasped them tightly and pressed them to her heart. She didn't hear his footsteps withdraw or the sound of crackling paper, or his frantic revelation, "There's a note, Emma; there's a note inside the bag!" He shook her more vigorously than he intended, waving the piece of paper in front of her tear-stained face. "Emma, it's a note; I think it's from your ex-boyfriend." His eyes scrutinised the paper. "Yes, yes; it's from Peter."

Slowly, Gary's words and the paper wafting in her face registered, making her wipe the tears away with her trembling fingers; making her water-filled eyes rise to the note in his hand. "What is it?" She narrowed her eyes. "Read it," she stated coldly.

"Are you sure?" He cocked one questioning eyebrow.

"Read it!" She snapped, her mouth set in a firm thin line; the upper part of her torso heaving heavily, though the salty tears had now dissipated.

Slowly, his fingers unfolded the paper, his eyes glaring at the scripted words, quickly taking in the substance of the message. As he raised his cautious eyes, they locked with ice-cold eyes staring directly at him. "Read it for Christ's sake, Gary," she demanded between clenched teeth, a new surge of mixed anger and frustration starting to bubble within her.

Taking a deep, ragged breath he began, his eyes focusing intermittently between the note in his hand and his girl, back to the note and finally resting on Emma, the words dying on his lips.

"What is it?" Her bemused eyes stared at him.

His eyes flitted erratically from Emma to the note in his hand and back to Emma. "It's Peter; he's-he's…in there." His forefinger pointed directly to the urn, where her incredulous eyes darted. "Peter is in that urn; or, at least, parts of him."

Her fast-beating heart instantly turned into a block of ice; dead like the ashes inside the urn. Horrified eyes glared at the polished container. Conkers are that colour, she mused, her mind drifting to happier days, making her smile whimsically.

"Emma, did you hear me? Peter… Peter is inside that urn." Gary's voice had risen an octave, together with his consternation; his brow furrowing, wondering what on earth had got into her for, by now, he half expected her to be jumping up and down in a mad frenzy, or on the floor flat out and dead to the world; instead, she seemed to be in her own distant world.

Crouching down beside her, with their uninvited *guest* between them, Gary placed both his firm hands on Emma's arms and looked directly into her distant eyes. "Emma, love," he said softly, "a little bit of Peter Brooke is inside this urn. Would you like me to read the note to you?"

What seemed like aeons passed by. Slowly, Emma's eyes wandered to the urn and remained there staring and disbelieving, while sharp shards of mixed emotions jabbed at her confused, whirling mind; twirling, whirling, stamping erratically around until all became a blurry mass, her unblinking eyes staring unblinkingly at the receptacle.

"Would you like me to read this?" He asked in a firmer tone, making her shift her glazed eyes to him.

She nodded.

"Are you sure?" Now that he had got her consent he was rethinking the idea.

Silently, she nodded her head once more.

He began.

Dear Emma,

Yes, you were once dear to me, if only for a brief spell in my life, and now my life is no more.

It's a long story, so I won't bore you with the details. Suffice it to say, you hurt me, Emma. It wasn't the fact that you were, and probably still are a hopeless flirt; after all, I admit, I was no saint myself. What hurt was the fact that I was replaced by a dog; a dog! I would have kind of, under duress, accepted the notion of another guy, but a pooch—

You know, Emma, I think we could have made it work; two wrongs, I feel, sometimes do make a right. However, as the saying goes, there is no point in crying over spilt milk.

Anyway, Fluffball has now departed to that doggie heaven in the sky. If you want a bit of him, read the enclosed note.

Keep flirting, Emma. It suits your character.

Peter x.
PS I'm sending you a bit of me for old times' sake.

She took the attached note and read the details of the forthcoming memorial. "I'll be there," she stated through clenched teeth, throwing eyes of disdain at the urn; her eyes rapidly glassing over, making Gary silently wonder whether his beau was grieving for her beloved Fluffball, or for Peter Brooke.

Tracy And Jade

"The trouble with Peter Brooke is Peter Brooke," Jade stated locking eyes with her best friend, Tracy.

"But I love him, Jade." Tracy's beseeching eyes lingered helplessly on her friend, willing her to step down from her judgemental pedestal and give Peter a chance.

"He's a good-for-nothing bum."

"I thought, you thought, he was a good-for-nothing flirt."

"That too," stated Jade nonchalantly.

"You won't even give him a chance, Jade."

"And you give him far too many chances, Tracy. Why isn't he here?"

"He's obviously been detained." Tracy rose from the sofa and approached the window, drew the lace curtain to one side and peered out onto the empty street, giving a resigned sigh.

"Or derailed; he's probably in some floozy's bed as we speak, Tracy. Why are you so damned blinkered? Anyway," she rose and gathered up the empty mugs and biscuit barrel, "are we going to *Bruno's*, or not?"

"Not."

"Not?"

"Not."

"Why not?"

"Pete's not here yet and if he comes and finds me gone then—"

"Then," interrupted Jade, a heavy tinge of impatience in her voice. "He'll move on to his next victim. Are you coming?"

Tracy turned her back on her old friend and pulled the closed curtain aside once more, her disappointed eyes witnessing the same scene with one difference, an elderly passing cyclist. When she looked back, her eyes rested on an empty room.

Jade walked briskly on, refusing to turn back or slow down her pace; refusing to acknowledge the caller until, eventually, Tracy caught up and both walked briskly on in unison, wrapped in their own blanket of silent contemplation, with one thought in both their minds; Peter Brooke.

Peter Brooke was a thorn in their midst; an irritating blister, in Jade's point of view, who would not go away. According to Tracy, he was a flirty delight, who brightened up her day and she fervently wished he would brighten up her nights too. Unbeknown to all three of them, he was a guy about to threaten the girls' friendship.

Bruno's was packed out; nothing unusual for a Friday night but, this night, it did not suit either girl's brooding mind. The casual flirts; the self-obsessed Casanovas; the know-it-alls; the vain creatures and self-seekers reminding Jade of the guy she couldn't stand while, simultaneously, reminding Tracy of the guy she so desperately craved to see, praying the door would open and he would casually stride into the crowded bar.

Peter Brooke possessed the characteristics Jade abhorred and Tracy adored. He was a male social butterfly and a flirt. His long-standing girlfriend, Amy Pilkington, put up with him, not because she loved him, but because she loved his good looks, his money and his popularity. Without those three essential ingredients, she knew only too well, he would be like all the other guys; a bore; a *nothing* and so she clung on to him like a desperate leech until the day she found a better offering.

Tracy Mason had fallen under Peter Brooke's bewitching spell, the minute she clapped eyes on him; hook line and sinker she was truly mesmerised and Peter Brooke was well aware of her adulation; he'd seen it all before and so he simply added her on to his, soon-to-be, list of conquests.

Conquests were the name of the game for Peter but sometimes, he quickly learned, they came with their own set of unique problems and complications. To contend with there were the betrayers; the already taken goods; the self-obsessed females who required high maintenance; the gold-diggers; the green-eyed monsters; the needy and the liars. He could go on and on listing inadequacies; he'd encountered them all in some form or other but a beautiful, intelligent, modest woman he was yet to find; though he thought as he placed one foot in front of the other, he might have already found her; if only it wasn't for her infuriating friend, who seemed to latch on to him like a desperate limpet.

She saw him walk in and abruptly turned her back on him, engaging the barman in casual chit-chat.

She saw him stride in and her fast-pulsating heart leapt and soared to the highest heavens as she silently stated, I knew he wouldn't let me down; I knew Jade was spouting off rubbish. Well, it's either that or she's jealous.

His mere presence made her insides squirm.

His mere presence made her heart flutter, dance and melt with love for him. Her smile widened and he responded.

"Hi, girls."

"Hi, Peter," squealed Tracy.

"Hi, Jade." His words now were more pronounced, making sure she'd heard him above the clanking glasses, jovial laughter and loud chatter.

She heard him and reluctantly turned to face him, forcing a well-practised smile, while inside she continued to squirm, her stomach churning furiously, for what Tracy saw in this flirtatious imbecile, she failed to see. All she managed to see was a numpty of the highest calibre.

Tracy nudged in closer; just the mere feel of him, standing so close to her, sent delightful shivers up and down her spine like a lively electrical current.

Full to the brim with finely tuned self-assurance, Peter Brooke was oblivious to Jade's negativity towards him; her pinned smile was enough to indicate that she was playing hard to get. Oh yes, she was interested. After all, he smirked nudging closer to the object of his desire, who wouldn't be?

As she edged closer, Tracy felt her fast-palpitating heart about to explode with sheer excitement. Rising her lovelorn eyes to him, her heart momentarily stopped. His eyes were elsewhere and, as she followed his gaze, the beats of her heart turned to envious thudding, for he was blatantly staring at—Jade; her best friend and her secret rival. Her eyes mesmerised; she stared at the source of her jealousy, while all around glasses clinked and tipsy revellers laughed and time stood still.

"What on earth is up with you, Tracy?" Jade chuckled. "You look as if you're staring at a ghost."

"Come on, Tracy love, I'll take you outside for a breath of fresh air," volunteered Peter.

They sat on a rustic bench facing the small car park, his protective arm around her shoulders, while they watched rowdy revellers heading off into town; others enjoying a cigarette; one pair snogging their mouths off; some heading off to private parties, while a tangled web of emotions weaved in Tracy's head.

Surreptitiously he glanced sideways at the woman sitting next to him; his eyes lingering on her dark, shoulder-length tresses, her face partly obscured by her satin-like hair; his eyes seeing another; his heart wishing it was the *other* he was gazing at and yearning to be with. "Are you all right now, Tracy; should we make a move back inside?" His words were hurried and impatient, complimenting his surging need to hasten inside and be close to the woman he desired.

"I want to go home, Peter," she stated each word clearly and concisely, making his heart instantly sink.

"Why don't we go inside," he encouraged, "maybe a fruit juice would…"

"I don't want a frigging fruit juice," she snapped, then added a blatant lie. "I don't feel well. I want you to take me home." Her eyes were stark and demanding, like her voice; firmly fixed on the man she adored; the man, she felt, was slipping away from her.

"What about Jade? We'll have to tell her."

"Now!"

"What about Jade?" He queried, hope lacing his words.

"She's old enough to fend for herself, Peter; she most certainly does not need you," retorted Tracy in cold, detached words; merciless and unfeeling; her tone venomous and spiteful.

They walked side by side, yet poles apart; one mentally clinging on to the other for dear life, for she felt she could not live without him; she would, she dismally concluded, be unable to breathe, function, survive without the thought of Peter Brooke being in her life.

A deep sense of being short-changed surged through and rooted itself in Peter's mind. He had imagined securing himself the grand prize this evening; instead, he found himself with the booby prize. His determined steps, as he walked side by side with his second-rate booty, belied his inner feelings, but he had a plan. He would ditch Tracy as soon as it was humanly possible to do so and he would rush back to *Bruno's* to claim his ultimate prize, Jade Cox.

Once inside the small, tastefully furnished flat, Peter watched incredulously as Tracy miraculously revived, making his blood surge and boil with undiluted fury, for now, he realised this had all been some sort of cunning ruse to get him on his own. His cold eyes darted to the source of his scorn and there they rested, while she bustled over to the drinks cabinet, poured out two generous measures of neat brandy, and planted her trim body as close to his as she dared while, inwardly he continued to seethe and writhe, while Jade's image danced vividly in his mind.

"Cheers," chirped Tracy clinking her glass with his and, while he gulped down his measure in one swallow, she brought her glass up to her lips, sipped and dreamed, while the clock on the wall chimed the hour, alerting Peter to the fact that if he wanted to catch Jade he better move; now!

"I better go, Tracy." He rose abruptly; the sound of the empty glass on the coffee table reverberating loudly in her ears, as her hopeful heart deflated.

"Stay," she lightly touched his arm with the tips of her fingers, "please."

He hated needy women; women who needed to beg. "Tracy, I have to go; it's late and there's work tomorrow." He stated firmly, his eyes avoiding her.

"Please stay, Peter."

"I have an important board meeting in the morning," he lied through his teeth, his eyes following her as she reached the drinks cabinet and procured two replenished brandy balloons.

"Just one more—please, Pete."

He knew she had a hidden agenda; it was as clear as day. Get him tipsy; get him into bed and have her wicked way with him, and ordinarily, he would have succumbed; in fact, that had been his own agenda before he had clapped eyes on Tracy's best friend. The second he had spotted Jade, his flirtatious heart had swapped allegiance. He wanted her and he immediately decided that he was going to have her. He did not know how. There was one major obstacle in the way, Tracy, and, since she and Jade were the best of friends as well as flatmates, that was one massive problem to solve.

Resignedly, he sank back into the sofa and took a gulp of brandy, closing his eyes and allowing the fiery liquid to slide down his throat, as his mind drifted back to the first time he encountered Jade when…she walked into the flat, wisps of blonde hair delectably escaping her chignon; her powder-blue suit doing justice to her trim figure and her shapely legs; her face radiating beauty and elegance; her lips partly open in surprise as she had not expected a visitor. "Hi." She smiled, barely acknowledging him, as she wandered into the kitchen and flicked on the kettle.

It was not the kind of reaction he expected from a new acquaintance. Normally he watched, with a great sense of satisfaction and a good deal of amusement, as they shrank in his presence. This beauty, he concluded, couldn't care less if he was the King of Siam. He wondered, listening to her happily humming away to herself, what it would be like to get this chick into the sack.

"Coffee?" She popped her head out the kitchen door. "Eh, I'm sorry, I don't know your name."

"Pete, it's Peter and he's just going," Tracy chirped.

"I'll stay for another coffee," contradicted Peter, his eyes glued on Jade.

From that moment on, it had been a personal ongoing losing battle to get Jade on her own and, for the time being, he made do with second best…

The touch of Tracy's body next to his brought him back sharply into the here and now. The soothing drink, the soft background music and lighting; a good-looking woman by his side, making seductive advances, made his emotions whirl erratically out of control. Jade can wait, he told himself, there will always be tomorrow. Placing the empty glass onto the coffee table, he took Tracy into his arms and suffused her with a heavy infusion of kisses. Within seconds, they were tearing frantically at each other's clothes until a jacket, blouse, tie, bra, skirt and trousers were all haphazardly abandoned on the floor, where they found themselves amongst their discarded belongings, as they explored each other's mouth with their eager tongues; exploring each other's bodies with their excited fingers while they sighed, gasped, thrust and exploded into splays of burning ecstasy.

"Oh, my God!"

They had been oblivious to the door clicking open and a pair of feet walking inside; too wrapped up in each other, they failed to see shocked eyes staring at their entangled, naked bodies.

From somewhere, deep in the depths of his ecstatic consciousness, he had heard the faint echoes of three words and his world of pleasure came tumbling down around him. Withdrawing, he scrabbled frantically into his trousers, zipping the fly before he dared to meet a pair of amused eyes, feeling the colour drain from his face and the horror enter his eyes.

There she was; his goddess. An overwhelming rush of bitter regret ruthlessly invaded his body, soul, mind and heart, for he knew Jade would never be able to un-see what she had just witnessed; never! He watched as her amused eyes switched to her friend, Tracy, whom, incidentally, he had completely forgotten about. His eyes followed Jade's eyes where they glared bitterly at the cause of his downfall.

Within minutes, he had walked out of their door and out of their lives.

Meredith

He found himself begrudgingly approaching the imposing building, he had not ventured in since childhood days, and then only under duress. Still, he told himself, he was on a crusade and needs must. His eyes drifted to and rested briefly on the dark stone construction and rose to the sun-dazzled, leaded glass windows and the solid oak door, wondering whether to turn and run in the opposite direction. His eyes were not focused on the door of a dentist's surgery, or the formidable door leading into the room of a truculent head teacher, yet his knees quivered and his feet were turning to jelly with the sheer anticipation of it all, for this was not an establishment he either cared about or had any interest in; in fact, books were the last thing on his mind and yet, here he was standing outside the local library. Needs must, he kept repeating in his head over and over again; a bet was a bet. Never in his life had he run away or shirked from a challenge, especially one that involved a member of the opposite sex; his reputation would never entertain the notion of defeat. The bet, he now concluded, had been a stupid idea, sealed after a session of excessive drinking. His mind drifted to the situation which had brought him here, as his feet involuntarily walked towards his destination…

"Come on, Pete; have another drink."

He had another and another and—another until everything around him became a fuzzy whirl.

The shrill continuous ringing of the phone drilled mercilessly into Peter's head, filtering into consciousness. "Yeah?" He snapped, his own voice reverberating ruthlessly in his aching head, mingled with the sound of chuckling drifting through the line.

"I hope you haven't forgotten that bet, mate," Tommy's words came through loud and clear.

He had forgotten and now it was, to his dismay, all coming back to him, as his friend continued enthusiastically. "So, my friend, you have to totter up to the chief librarian, chat her up and ask her out on a date. I need solid proof, mate; otherwise, no money."

Peter Brooke couldn't care less about the money, he had enough money to last a lifetime; but a bet, well that was a totally different matter altogether. In Peter Brooke's book, it was sacrilege to renegade on a bet…

He stood at the door pondering on the ornate carving, unable to identify what it actually depicted. With a heavy heart, he pushed the door open and walked in. Step by step his footsteps reverberated loudly in his ears, as he walked along the well-trodden wooden floor. Where he was going, he hadn't a clue. Onwards he ventured approaching a set of glass doors and walking through he came upon a sign in black bold lettering, *Information.* Within seconds, he was escorted by an efficient-looking, middle-aged woman into the main body of the library, his eyes rapidly scanning rows upon rows of books of all sizes and thicknesses on long shelves. He'd always detested reading; wondered what the point of it was when he could get all the news, information and forms of escapism from the television set. Step by step, he followed the efficient-looking professional, a sudden coughing fit attacking him, followed by a series of admonishing stares thrown his way, from the tops of stuffy-looking tomes and open newspapers. "S…sorry," he stuttered.

"Shh!" came the harsh reply.

He listened half-heartedly, to the areas where he could locate various genres of literature and where to go for specific snippets of information. "Where do I find the head librarian?" He interrupted the woman's flow of words, with only one thing on his mind.

The woman bestowed on him a forced smile. "You shall find Miss Enderby in that area." Her straight, thin finger pointed to the far end of the large room. "Will that be all, sir?"

If only, he mused wistfully, nodding his head. "Yes…yes, that will be all; thank you." He lowered himself into a chair and closed his tired eyes, his head pounding; wishing to God he was anywhere else but in this damned hell of hell.

After minutes of blissful oblivion, he opened his exhausted eyes and allowed them to wander around the spacious room. How anyone in their right mind could spend their time in this hole was beyond his imagination; five minutes in this ghastly place was more than enough. Still, a bet was a bet and the sooner he got it over and done with, the sooner he could forget about the whole blasted thing. Suddenly his eyes lit up, his heart giving a wild flip. Perhaps, this wasn't such a damned hell-hole after all, he mused, his eyes resting on a young head popping up from behind the head librarian's desk. Maybe, he thought, this is not such a bad bet and, licking his upper lip in anticipation, he rose and took steps towards the formidable-looking desk. She turned; he gaped. "Yes, can I help you, sir?"

Yes; you most certainly can help me, Miss Enderby, he answered silently, his lips twitching in admiration of what he saw before him.

"Sir, can I be of any assistance?" The young librarian cut into his lascivious thoughts, as his eyes took in an unblemished face; wide, innocent-looking eyes and lips, so warm and inviting. "Sir!"

He witnessed a shapely eyebrow rising in question. "Erm…yes…erm… Have you anything on the Second World War?" He answered with a subject that randomly popped into his head.

"What particular aspect are you interested in?"

He stared mesmerised as her luscious lips moved opening and closing, opening and closing. "Erm…any," he answered nonchalantly.

"Any?"

"Any?"

"Please follow me, sir."

He followed her like a faithful puppy, drinking in her curvy figure attired in a navy blue suit. Not designer, he assessed. Still, it did justice to her well-proportioned figure. Shame about the flat shoes, he mused, picturing her shapely legs in a pair of stilettoes.

"Here we have…"

He didn't hear the rest his head whirling, twirling and hastily making dating plans. By the time he had looked up, she had disappeared and he was staring bemusedly at a set of books, dealing with the Battle of Britain. His eyes flitted here, there and everywhere; the chief librarian was nowhere in sight. The soft vibration of his mobile propelled his hand to grab his phone, his eyes dropping to scan the message… *And, don't even think about substituting the woman if she happens to resemble a gorgon, mate…* He shut his phone off, stuffed it deep into his jacket pocket and went on a searching mission.

Drumming his fingers on the orderly desk his eyes widened as a figure, twice the age of the one he was expecting to see, came into full view. "Yes, can I help?"

He heard the echo of her words. "I would like to speak to the head librarian."

"I am the head librarian."

"Miss Enderby?"

Her brow furrowed; her lips formed into a firm, disciplined line as she nodded her head; her shrewd eyes scanning carefully the suspicious-looking character standing before her.

He felt his heart drain, shrink and sink into the depths of despair, as his puzzled eyes continued to glare questioningly at the formidable-looking female before him. A typical librarian, he thought; a stern-faced creature, primly suited and booted, with a pair of horn-rimmed spectacles, perched on the end of her crooked nose for good measure. Yuk! But; how to get out of this dastardly bet?

Sharp words brought him out of his dismal reverie and his eyes back into sharp focus. "Sir, is there anything I can do for you?"

"Are you sure you're Miss Enderby?" The second the words popped out of his mouth, he realised how absolutely ludicrous they sounded.

"No, I am the Queen of Sheba," she replied scathingly. She turned her straight back on him, leaving him to ponder further on his own stupidity, but not for long as a mischievous idea sprang into his head and a victorious smile slid onto his lips. Tommy, he concluded, would never know.

Lady Luck was on his side. As he was musing on his delightful plan, the young librarian seemed to have appeared out of nowhere and was engaged in deep conversation with the chief, Miss Enderby, both women throwing Peter surreptitious glances. He'd seen it all before; he was a babe magnet and women of all ages; all creeds and colours couldn't help but be drawn towards him. That was, he mused, the undisputed charm of Peter Brooke.

Now was the time to act. With bold steps he approached the tidy desk and two pairs of eyes swiftly darted to him, lips smiling condescendingly. He placed a hastily picked-up tome onto the desk. "A little light reading."

Eyebrows shoot up. "Adolf Hitler?"

His bemused eyes dropped to the book and stared at the stern-looking character looking up at him. He looked up and smiled foolishly.

The young woman shook her head from side to side, smiled at her chief and proceeded to hand out a library application form for Peter to fill in before he was allowed to take his *light* reading home.

As he completed the last segment of the application, he looked up. Their eyes met. "Can I take you out for a drink this evening, as a thank you for your services?" His words rushed out, his eyes not leaving the young woman's face.

"Why not?" She smiled.

Bruno's bar was, as usual, bursting at the seams, when Peter walked in and made a bee-line for Tommy at the crowded bar. "So," Tommy raised an eyebrow, "you pulled it off; you've got a date with the head librarian?"

"Sure have," beamed Peter, his green eyes twinkling, "just wait till you see her, mate."

"I can't wait." Tommy took a generous slug of beer and scanned the entrance, his heart beating in eager anticipation.

Revellers sauntered in and exited the smoky crowded bar, while two pairs of expectant eyes remained firmly fixed on the door. Finally, Tommy glanced at his watch and clapped his friend's shoulder. "Well, it looks as if you've been stood up, my friend." Draining the remnants of his beer, he enquired jovially, "Another; my round?"

"Why not?" Peter muttered nonchalantly, his eyes surveying the congested room; his eyes darting back and lingering on the entrance.

"There you go, mate." Tommy placed the glass of cool, dark, inviting liquid onto the bar mat, turning to his old-time friend. "Hey, it's not like you, Pete, to be stood up by a date; didn't you say eight o'clock?"

Peter's restless eyes flitted back to the entrance. "Yeah, eight-ish; half-eight; she'll turn up. I mean, man, how can she resist such temptation?" He smiled his devilish smile and picked up his beer. Taking a swill he turned to his friend. "Anyway, I thought you had a date; how long have you been seeing this chick now?"

"A while, she'll be here soon."

"And, you haven't given me the pleasure of seeing her for myself." Peter shook his head from side to side in mock disapproval.

"No, I haven't," came a short, sharp reply; for Tommy Eggleton knew Peter and his flirty ways and he knew his flirtations frequently led to a lot more; often to disappointment, betrayal, loss of friendship and broken hearts, not to mention irrevocably broken lives. "Oh shit! I forgot I'm meeting her at *Gino's* restaurant." Tommy swilled his drink in one go. "I'll have to leave you, mate." He patted Peter on his back and proceeded to push his way through the rowdy drinkers, leaving his friend to brood.

Only once in his life had Peter Brooke been stood up; he was fourteen and a half at the time. He glanced at his watch; eight thirty-seven. He ordered another beer and scanned the available, and not-so-available, talent; studying them all with an avid interest as he took in the young, the not so young; girls wearing skirts which barely covered their legs and backsides; others with long frocks to their ankles; females with glossy, straight, blonde hair and those with curly, black tresses; skinny frames and those of a more indulgent nature. They were all the same to him; any one of them would do, so long as he was not on his own. His eyes drifted to a redhead, surrounded by a group of friends and his green flinty eyes narrowed, as he studied her intently from afar. She seemed a popular figure; a girl who seemingly enjoyed a laugh and a drink, judging from her raucous laughter. His observant eyes soaked in her slim body, her long legs making his imagination run riot and the tip of his tongue lasciviously lick his upper lip. Placing his glass down, he placed one foot in front of the other.

"Mister Brooke?"

The echo of his name on unidentifiable lips made his attention divert from the redhead and irritation to surge through his blood, his eyes turning to saucers and shock waves to wash over him. "Missus…erm…" Swiftly he turned back to the redhead; she was not looking his way. His incredulous eyes stared at the woman standing before him.

"Miss Enderby is the name, Mister Brooke."

His disbelieving eyes continued to stare starkly at the stern-faced, primly suited woman and decided she looked no more appealing after three beers, from when he last clapped eyes on her when he was stone-cold sober; in fact, he dismally concluded, she seemed to have aged ten years, which wasn't a great thing, as he had already pinned her down to being around sixty-ish. His mouth repeatedly opened and closed, resembling a goldfish; finally, words formulated into an incoherent sentence. "But…erm…em…but…the young lady…the other librarian…erm."

"Ah, Miss Baxter."

"Yes…yes, Miss Baxter," he stared inquisitively, hoping this ancient fossil would shed light on the matter.

"Miss Baxter had her fingers crossed behind her back; saw you coming from a mile off and wanted to teach a flirt like you a lesson, Mister Brooke," Miss Enderby announced without any scruples on her part.

His hard eyes widened in utter amazement, creating a line across his brow. "What do you mean; a flirt like me, Miss Enderby?" Then decided not to pursue this line of questioning stating icily, "A date is a date; doesn't Miss Baxter possess any manners?"

"You have a date, Mister Brooke." Miss Enderby swiped off her horn-rimmed spectacles and pinned on the sweetest smile she could muster, making his whole insides wrench and his incredulous eyes blink rapidly.

"You!" He gasped and spluttered.

She watched the *worm* squirm, replacing her glasses back onto her crooked nose to acquire a clearer view of her victim. "I am your date, Mister Brooke. Meredith didn't want you to go without, so to speak; so, here I am; ready and willing."

Peter Brooke stood transfixed as if in a haze, a name swimming round and round in his confused head—*Meredith*—Not a name one comes across every day. And, suddenly, it struck him; didn't Tommy once reluctantly mention his new girlfriend was called Meredith?

"Meredith," the name involuntarily escaped his mouth.

"Yes, Meredith; Miss Baxter's Christian name is Meredith, Mister Brooke."

Miss Enderby's words reverberated loudly in his head, pounding and beating within the confines of his skull, swimming round and round—round and round. Swiftly he turned his back on his date. "Double vodka," he snapped at the barman, while Miss Enderby tut-tutted and rested her eyes of sheer disgust on him. Slithering down his throat, the clear liquid provided him with a few moments of calm and clarity. Meredith; yes the name was familiar to him; Tommy had definitely mentioned a Meredith, but he could have been talking about a distant cousin, his neighbour, a pet spider. Surely, he told himself, it would be too coincidental for Tommy to be going out with Meredith Baxter. If only he had listened more attentively to what his friend had been jabbering on about.

"Are you all right, Mister Brooke?"

Gradually everything came back into focus; the crowded pub, the not-too-cheerful barman, the rowdy partygoers and pleasure seekers; his eyes resting reluctantly on the sour-faced woman before him; his date.

"Are you all right?" She repeated. "You look on the pale side."

He nodded distractedly into space.

"Then, your manners are clearly not," she announced loudly and clearly, her no-nonsense tone forcing his reluctant eyes to focus on the odious woman while seeing only her young colleague, the girl he thought he was going to date; the girl he thought—He snapped his eyes shut, opened them and stated, "I've got to go."

50

"Meredith thought that this would teach you a lesson; flirtatious men deserve…"

He didn't hear the rest as he placed one determined foot in front of the other, pushing his way through the jovial crowd until he came to a sudden stop.

Eyes met eyes; met eyes and two mouths burst out into uncontrollable, spontaneous laughter, while one mouth opened like a gaping cavern, blood surging wildly through Peter's veins, his mind reeling in all directions and his feet feeling like two solid blocks, unable to move a mere centimetre, while echoes of laughter invaded, penetrated and permeated his hazy, buzzing head. "M… Meredith!" His stark eyes stared unflinchingly at the laughing female, he thought he had arranged a date with; the female who was Tommy's date. His disbelieving eyes drifted to his friend, who was beaming from ear to ear, having been in on the joke from the start and now deeming it safe enough to introduce his girl to Peter. "Meredith," Peter repeated as if it was the only word he possessed in his vocabulary armoury.

"Sorry." Giggled the young woman, trying desperately to stifle another escaping chuckle. "I thought it would be a laugh; I thought…"

"I know what you thought," he cut in. "Your chief told me what you thought. Well, I don't happen to think it's in the least bit funny. Now, if you don't mind." He proceeded to walk on.

"Oh, come on, mate." Tommy placed a firm hand on Peter's shoulder. "You must admit, the whole charade is quite humorous." He giggled unable to control himself. "By the way, what do you think of the lovely Miss Enderby?" He cocked a mischievous eyebrow, the edge of his mouth quivering.

Peter's eyes in his poker face darted back to the laughing librarian and, at that split moment, he thought she looked twenty years younger. Shaking his incredulous head at the audacity of it all, he turned and proceeded to leave once more.

"Please don't go, Peter," said Meredith, touching lightly his arm with her fingers.

It was something in her soft, warm voice; something, in the feather-touch of her fingers on his arm, which made his feet stop moving.

"Please," she urged.

There it was again, that gentle voice, he mused. Like a siren luring him into succumbing to her will.

"I'd like to get to know you."

He felt his senses, his body; his mind, soul and heart drowning—melting—melting—drowning in her soft, dulcet words as he revelled in his own weakness.

"Tommy has told me so much about you." She smiled, her eyes twinkling.

Yeah, I bet he has and he hasn't told me a darned thing about you, honey. Peter silently acknowledged. His eyes melted in the softness of her blue eyes and, again, he felt himself drowning; immersing himself in a sea of envy which lapped over his mind, washed over his jealous heart and threatened to destroy him in its destructive element. It was a raging, merciless sea that was only content in revelling in its own ferocious power, no matter who it crushed along the way.

As they sat around the small table with its assortment of drinks, empty crisp packets, a mobile and a set of car keys, the ravaging sea thrashed and roared, propelling the green-eyed monster to ask, *Why him; why Tommy; why not me?* His envious eyes lingered on his best mate and his girl; hating Tommy and hating the girl sitting between them; hating the obnoxious Miss Enderby, and above all, hating himself for he had wanted Meredith from the first time he had set eyes on the young, attractive librarian; he had wanted her then and now he wanted this forbidden fruit more than ever and as the mighty, powerful, raging sea within him threatened to destroy everything, he secretly vowed, *she will be mine*, as his jealous eyes followed their every move; the surreptitious meeting of their eyes; the not-so-accidental touch of their fingers; the closeness of their bodies; the way they ended each other's sentences, as if they already knew each other inside out; their discreet, but oh so obvious, hints of making their escape and their subtle, but of so clear impatience of others hindering their intentions, as they forcibly pinned on resigned smiles making Peter's guts twist and wrench as a fresh bout of deep, dangerous hatred for his old friend surged violently and uncontrollably through every fast-pulsating vein, his eyes focused on the object of his desire, who was totally unaware of his intense scrutiny. *I am going to have you, Meredith*, he swore. *By hook or by crook, you will be mine.*

"Another drink everyone; my round?" Tommy tore himself away from Meredith's side, collecting the empties while Peter nodded, firmly positioned in his own private hell, his eyes remaining locked on the girl of his best friend.

"It was a laugh; don't you agree, Peter?" Miss Enderby broke his destructive reverie with her shrill voice, like a sharp fingernail scratched along a blackboard slicing through his consciousness, forcing him to tear his eyes away from his challenge and look at the older woman. He squeezed a smile and nodded his head obligingly, his eyes quickly reverting back to Meredith, while his mind furiously weaved a plan and, like the raging sea within him, it was cataclysmic, for someone undoubtedly would be destroyed.

Two minds were oblivious to each other's plight; two minds had one blissful thought, Meredith. She was in the centre of their conscious and unconscious minds and always in the starring role. But there was one major difference; one mind was focused on a long-term, stable relationship; and the other absorbed in a selfish, destructive goal. Both sets of challenges were set in the opposing minds of two best pals.

Meredith was conscious only of the present and the present involved only Tommy Eggleton. Since meeting her soulmate, she had resided in a blissful heaven and aimed to remain there forever. She smiled. Tommy seemed happy with the way their relationship was progressing too. Her smile extended at the thought of her new friend, Peter. The *incident,* she mused, had been so funny and he seemed to be such a good sport, taking their innocent joke as a bit of light-hearted fun. Yeah, she silently concluded, my Tommy has certainly got himself a good mate.

Peter's regular visits to the library were to begin with unexpected, but as time progressed, Meredith looked forward to the door opening and Peter sauntering through. Peter, she had decided, was so like her boyfriend and yet so very different. Both men, she mused, had a good sense of humour and cared for and respected her. Tommy made sure she was treated like a lady, appreciated her in every way, and would do anything for her; Peter, on the other hand, was proving to be a very good friend, a great listener; someone, she thought, she could rely on in times of trouble.

Trouble came to pass a month after she had been acquainted with Peter and her reliance on him changed three lives forever.

Tommy's beloved father was dying, and after a lot of soul searching, it was decided that Tommy would go over to Ireland and help tend to his father's palliative care and say his broken-hearted *goodbye* to the man he loved so dearly. Meredith declined the invitation. It was, she secretly concluded, a precious father-son time. She refused to be the third wheel.

Tommy's broken heart splintered in many directions, and as he departed for the Emerald Isle, he reluctantly placed his girlfriend in his friend's protective care.

Peter's word was his bond; at least, that's how it set out to be. His interest in Meredith had not quelled; still, he vowed to have her but not in these dire set of circumstances; not when his best buddy's father was breathing his last; not when his grieving friend had placed his broken-hearted trust in him; not when the situation proclaimed loudly and clearly to him that this was a no-no situation. Other times would surely come; this was definitely not the time.

Visits to the library, specifically to see Meredith, continued to be friendly, light-hearted and supportive for Peter Brooke knew he had to gain Meredith's ultimate trust; his view on the matter, however, did change with the extended length of Tommy's absence. Secretly, Peter bestowed on himself the role of guardian; like a guardian angel, making sure his charge was protected, cared for and happy.

As she could not drive, he took her to the supermarket once a week, occasionally escorted her on a walk to the park, accompanied her on an evening to the cinema, joined her in a casual drink in the local pub; he took over Tommy's role with one important exception; he did not bed the woman he was secretly lusting after. That, he mused, would have to wait; but, he determined, it would happen when Tommy was back at home and had grieved sufficiently; when he was strong enough to cope with losing his girl to his best mate.

The persistent ringing of the phone alerted Peter, demanding his attention. His heart leapt when he heard her voice then rapidly deflated. "What on earth is it, Meredith?" Her sob-laden words told him the sad news, Tommy's father had died, and with the news, a heavy foreboding filled Peter's heart. His friend would be coming home and reclaiming what was his; soon he would be the third wheel again.

Peter's heart soared. Tommy was not coming home, after all; at least, not for the time being. He had decided to remain in Ireland to sort out his father's estate and affairs. He was not going to be the spare part, after all, he smiled satisfactorily. A fresh bout of heart-wrenching sobs brought him swiftly back to the here and now. "He's not coming back, Peter. What am I going to do without my Tommy?"

He seized his chance. "I am coming over." He answered and put down the phone before she could decline his statement. Quickly checking himself in the mirror, giving his curly hair a hasty run-through with his fingers, he dabbed a dash of expensive cologne onto his face, picked up a couple of condoms, grabbed his car keys and slammed the door hard behind him.

The door opened on a sobbing, miserable figure and within seconds she was cradled in his strong arms feeling a warm, comforting blanket of security and protection around her. It wasn't Tommy, she closed her tearful eyes, but she could pretend it was; they were not Tommy's protective arms around her; it was not Tommy's soft, reassuring voice telling her everything was going to be all right; it was not his soft hair brushing against her temple; or his warm, inviting lips claiming her mouth, but she could pretend it was and while she pretended, the world seemed a better place. "Oh, Tommy… Tommy… Tommy…" She whispered softly in between glorious, deep-tongued kisses. "Tommy…" She sighed feeling as if she was drowning in a warm pool of love; feeling all her anxieties ebbing away under the fervent pressure of his mouth; overpowered by his warmth, his longing, his need, as they drained away her pent-up emotions that had been so long in check and she yielded to him.

She felt like putty in his hands, he could do with her what he willed; his fingers running through her hair freeing her long, blonde tresses from a chignon so that they fell around her shoulders like a mantle; his urgent mouth claiming her mouth, her cheeks, her slender neck as his fingers followed suit tracing her fine neck down—down to the tip of her blouse, where he deftly undid the buttons one by one, unclasping her lacy bra and releasing her breasts from their prison. She felt his cool lips around one nipple then another as his tongue teased them into rigidity, making her gasp and sigh and cry, "Oh Tommy… Tommy…"

His friend's name drifted through his consciousness like a distant echo; just like Tommy, far away. He was here; Peter Brooke was here. Peter Brooke was her lover.

At that moment in time, she was blind to her lover's identity, lost in her fantasy and he was only conscious of his needs, greedy and self-absorbed; conscious only of the burning passion running through him like a live electrical current.

Discarded clothes laying randomly abandoned on the floor, they lay beside them in the deflating aftermath of their lovemaking; two pairs of eyes staring starkly at the ceiling; two racing hearts subsiding in their wild hammering, as the here and now seeped gradually into their consciousness; filtering in and taking over, dispelling any remnants of need, fantasy, thrills, excitement and replacing them with stark, raw reality and—guilt.

Her guilty eyes, the loose touch of her fingers around his neck, the lack of warmth as they stood in the arrivals area, told a bereaved Tommy all that he needed to know.

Silence heavy, thick and overbearing covered them as Tommy and Meredith stared at anything and anyone but each other, seeing only a black future without the other and in the midst of it all, like the proverbial elephant in the room, was Peter Brooke; the destructive knife that had destroyed their relationship and their future. His name was never mentioned; it was taboo.

Peter Brooke was aware of the emotional destruction he had left in his wake; he had seen it all before, chose to ignore it and swiftly moved on to his next victim.

Seven Years Later

Slowly, she closed the door on her unexpected visitor, and holding the mysterious package in her hand, moved towards the window, held back the net curtain and watched as the figure retreated out of the drive and out of sight, the *click-click-click* of her stilettoes on the drive still echoing in Meredith's head. Allowing the curtain to fall she placed the package on to the kitchen table, made herself a coffee and opened a magazine, her eyes flitting inadvertently to the object on the table. It's something for Johnny, she thought. It usually was. Finishing her drink, she deposited the bulky item on to the coffee table and walked out the door.

Though it was secreted in brown paper, it was, from what she had determined, a strangely shaped object, and as she walked along the paved drive, the echo of the stranger's stilettoes continued to bombard her head. It was, she thought, an unusual delivery. Who was this woman? Was she a teacher? Why had she simply despatched the offering on the doorstep, with just a simple quick knock on the door and without a single word of explanation spoken? Meredith shook her head. Strange; very, very strange, she mused. And the more she thought about it throughout the day, the more bizarre the whole thing became until it all became a massive, confusing blur and she turned her whole attention on to the library books in hand.

He sat rigid his young hands clasped around the package, wondering what on earth it could be, as excitement tingled through his young body. He went through the same ritual every time he received a parcel. He would sit with his hands on top or around the mysterious item before him and try and guess what it could be and usually, he was right. Today was different; he couldn't, for the life of him, hazard a guess as he sat perfectly still, his mind concentrating, his pulse racing, gingerly fingering the bulky, strange-shaped item imagining he was a blind boy determining the identity of an object by his sense of touch. The corner of his mouth twitched, his lips spreading into a delightful smile. It could be— wait a minute—He raised his fingers to the top once more. Maybe—a new pair of football boots in a strange container? He had been on about them for weeks and, although he knew his mum was not rolling in money, he also knew she did her best to provide for him. He gripped the container feeling its solidness; a tin? His brow furrowed. Maybe Miss Enderby had sent him some sweets, after all, it was a regular occurrence. Yes, he determined, it was a container full of sweets, or chocolates, or—moon rocks! Silently he congratulated himself on solving the mystery before the unveiling and now he was going to prove to himself, that he was indeed the genius he claimed to be.

Opening his eyes, his fingers carefully unwrapped the brown paper; around and around it went slowly revealing a brown, shiny base, a roundish middle and a most delightful-looking lid, with a solid bobble on the top. Most definitely sweets, he concluded, hoping they were his favourite toffees, already his mouth was watering. His eyes followed an envelope falling to the floor. No need to read the message, he already knew who the welcome treats were from. "Thank you, Miss Enderby," he said aloud and swiftly his eager fingers opened the top.

The silence and stillness of the small kitchen as she walked in immediately enveloped her in a blanket of uneasiness. Usually, there was the sound of the television, the radio or the bleeps transmitting from a computer game; this afternoon there was only eerie silence. Her puzzled eyes swept around the room and found everything as she had left it this morning; the sink sparkling clean, the worktops tidy and all the crockery in place and out of sight; everything quiet and spotless. Where was Johnny; he should be home by now. Her brow furrowed and relaxed. Was there an after-school football practise today? Her feet took hasty steps towards the American-style fridge where, amongst the colourful magnets and photos, was displayed a diary-type calendar, her eyes espying something on the table. Her feet stopped; her body perfectly still and turning rapidly to ice as her eyes glared, her mind whirling furiously and wondering what she was actually staring at, as her brow furrowed once more, creating perplexed lines across her forehead.

"What on earth!" She exclaimed aloud, as she took closer steps towards the object of her curiosity; inhaling a deep, ragged breath, as her eyes rested on the scattered contents and her guts writhed and twisted, a sickly nausea sweeping over her as her unblinking eyes stared.

Grabbing the nearest chair with her trembling fingers, she slumped down, her glaring eyes fixed on the brown, shiny container and its contents as cold, stark realisation began to seep into her muffled, flummoxed mind. Transfixed by the object, and what there was scattered around it, she dared not even contemplate what the stuff was, as she wondered who in this world could play such a sick, nasty joke. Staring and wondering her confused mind raced through all the people she knew; all the people she liked and all those she didn't, her mind lingering on former boyfriends.

Besides Tommy, the others were of no importance, she concluded, shaking her head slowly from side to side. And, Tommy would never stoop to such a low level. Yes, he had been hurt, even crushed by her, but deep in her heart of hearts, she knew Tommy still loved her; he would not hurt her in such a despicable way. Apart from Tommy, she mused, she had had only one more sexual experience with—Peter; Peter Brooke.

Quickly she gathered the grey grains into the urn, covered it with the brown paper and deposited it out of sight. A sick joke, like the pathetic troll that played it; that's all, she told herself over and over again. But, where was Johnny? The calendar had shown there was no after-school sporting session. So where the dickens was he?

The frantic search was fruitless. Rooms were empty, as was the back garden. His friends had not seen him since school ended. So where the heck had Johnny got to?

The shrill ring of the phone momentarily shook her out of her anxious thoughts; a heavy wave of relief washed over her. He was safe. She smiled. Johnny, her precious son, was safe. Her smile died on her lips as stark eyes stared into space; into another time long, long gone but never forgotten. Had the past finally caught up with her; was it staring her blatantly in the face and bestowing silent retribution?

Lowering on to a chair she closed her eyes and listened to time slipping away, the sudden chime forcing her eyes to open, her mind resuming its damning litany. Whoever it was playing this stupid game, he or she was sick; sick in the head and sick in heart, body and soul. Sick! From the corner of her eye, she espied a white item on the carpet, making her brow crease, as a shiver of raw apprehension surged through every vein in her body. Gingerly, she picked up the envelope, rumbling dread adding to the heavy weight of unease. An envelope, she concluded, signified a sender and a possible identification of the despicable troll. Her eyes stared at the envelope in her quivering fingers. "To Meredith," she read aloud, her words cold and detached, as if they were coming from a ghost of the past. She snapped her eyes shut, knowing that whoever the sender was, he or she wanted to hurt her.

The clock ticked laboriously marking the passage of time. Roughly tearing open the envelope, Meredith withdrew the paper inside, unfolded it and silently read.

'Meredith,

I am sorry for all the hurt I caused you.
Please forgive me.

Peter'

Fifteen words. She had slowly counted them one by one. Fifteen words and the last sentence pleaded for pardon, but it was the very last word, the name, which crushed her heart making her tortured guts wrench, twist, gnaw as every beat of her pounding heart refused to forgive, for how could she forgive what he had done; what she had done; what they had mutually done?

A merciless tight and icy band tugged, clawed and squeezed her heart as her eyes shifted to and starkly focused on the brown-shrouded vessel a sudden, sharp stab of new anxiety attacking her tortured heart, chilling her bones, transforming her surging blood into a frozen sheet of ice; her eyes stark, unflinching, staring. Without a grain of doubt, she knew what was inside the urn; the note had informed her of Peter Brooke's forthcoming memorial service.

The click of the door alerted her to the fact Johnny was home, his arrival bringing with it a heavy impending doom.

Mother and Son sat on opposite sides of the kitchen table; two islands invaded by an uninvited intruder, who was now between them like a dividing wedge while silence, reigning wholly and supremely, was punctuated only by the sound of the ticking clock.

"Is it moon dust, Mummy?" Johnny asked, his excited voice belying the inner doubt washing over him, as his hopeful innocent eyes unwaveringly lodged on his mother's pale face.

The clock ticked monotonously on.

"Mummy." His young eyes followed her head as it shook from one side to the other, her guilt-ridden eyes avoiding those of her son; her involuntary, dry lips uttering the words she never wanted to say, "It is your father." Her words were cold and detached, making the boy's eyes grow wider with ultimate incredulity. Her eyes switched to her son as she wrenched the rest of her words out of her heart, soul and mouth. "This is Peter, your biological father, Johnny; the father you never knew." She watched his body shift position on the chair, his smooth face screw up before a series of childish giggles burst forth, his young eyes darting to the urn and back to his mum in total disbelief. "This is your father," she repeated rising, scooping up the urn and shoving it into the cupboard, disallowing Peter Brooke's intrusion into their long overdue mother-son talk.

After the giggles had subsided, the boy listened attentively to every single word his mother said; his big, innocent eyes not leaving her for a split second and, when she had finished, he smiled. "Can I go out to play now, Mummy?"

A faint touch of a mother's smile flickered on her lips. "Yes, Son, you can go out and play." She picked up the paper, her eyes scanning the details of the memorial service and nodded silently, her lips grimly set.

Mary

He saw her from afar, alone, in the throes of grief and rather plain-looking, from what he could make out from his vantage point. His eyes moved on to more attractive females; some with partners; others with female companions and one or two on their own, his eyes drifting back to the solitary mourner, on the front pew next to the coffin; his mouth forming a wry smile. There was something— her vulnerability—her aloofness—her grief, something about her which mystified him, making his head move from side to side in puzzlement.

He watched her beneath hooded eyes as she stood demurely at the graveside, her intent eyes on the coffin as it slid further and further out of sight and stopped at its final resting place in the cold, damp earth. She was not his usual sort, he silently mused; his observant eyes scrutinising her plain, black, knee-length coat; her mousy coloured hair tied up in a ponytail which lay loosely on one side of her coat, a fringe covering her forehead; her face slim, pale, serious. Not a looker, he concluded, but there was *something* about her. He watched as she sprinkled the casket with a handful of earth; watched as she dabbed the tears on her face with a white laced handkerchief and watched her walk away in the opposite direction.

It was, he decided, her air of vulnerability and decorum; the air of old worldliness surrounding her which made her so interesting, so different, so very refreshing; that was the mysterious *something*. He turned and walked away, a fleeting regret sweeping over him. Shaking his head from side to side, he smiled at his own inconsistency. She was not his type, not by a very long chalk.

Winter turned into spring and folded into summer. Peter Brooke worked hard and played hard, constantly creating instant friends and lifelong enemies of both sexes in equal measures. He'd long ago lost count of the number of women he had bedded; the hearts he had broken; the lives he had inadvertently destroyed due to his selfish desires. He was aware only of his greedy need for a challenge which involved flirting, bedding and disposing of victims. He was totally unaware of the heartache he often caused and the heartbreak he was soon to experience for the very first time in his entire life.

Again, in church, he saw her. This time she was positioned in the middle of a pew, amidst a group of friends, as they eagerly waited for the grand arrival of their colleague and friend. It was, he concluded, undeniably the girl he had seen before; she was the only prim and proper-looking one; the one attired in a smart, green pastel dress, her hair tied back in a neat bun while the others showed off their designer frocks, garish accessories and their long, tumbling hair extensions topped with designer fasteners and elegant, wide-brimmed hats. The milliner, he mused, must have had a field day. His eyes switched back to the woman who stood out by her unique simplicity. Yep, she was different, he mused, and, although she was far removed from the outgoing females he usually pursued, he wanted her.

Watching intently as she stepped into the aisle and proceeded to walk forward, he silently deduced that she was going to Communion and therefore she was a Catholic. If she was a devout Roman Catholic then she would be a tough nut to crack, he mused, but one he surely could crack.

Mary Simpson proved to be a very hard nut to crack; his flannel, wit and charm allowed her the privilege of feeling she was the centre of attention; promising her the earth did nothing to give him the slightest speck of hope.

After much exasperated effort on his part, his unwilling feet followed her into church one morning, as she diligently partook in her routine of daily worship.

"How about a coffee?" He suggested after the Mass had ended. She smiled. He had caught her; he silently congratulated himself, revelling in his self-assured success.

"I am sorry, I can't." Her stiff smile remained on her lips as she walked off.

Eleven times he had asked her to join him for a coffee, or a walk in the park; eleven times she had made one excuse after another. But, one day, he smiled to himself, she would crumble. One day.

Unwillingly, he sauntered into the church once more and put in a request to a God he did not believe in and often scorned. Resignedly, he walked alone back to his expensive car and then, one day, he stopped going to the church; stopped putting in his futile requests and moved on to new and promising pastures.

Driving along the winding country roads, the top of his red convertible down, his free hand lingering enticingly on his on-off girlfriend, Amy Pilkington's, thigh; he took a sharp bend at top speed, abruptly his foot slamming on the brake pedal hard. "What the fucking hell?" His machine came to a sudden stop. "What the fucking hell are you thinking of stopping here?" He yelled as his door opened and slammed and he, and a stony-faced Amy, stood beside a clapped-out motor, a suspicious hissing sound exuding from within an opened bonnet; a perplexed figure standing glaring at the rising steam. The frustrated driver turned, feeling a presence.

"Oh, it's you," Peter's angry tone had rapidly transformed into a voice of surprise, edged with concern. "Are you all right?"

Amy Pilkington's eyes flitted from her boyfriend, to the stranger, and back to her beau. "Do you know her, Pete?" She asked, her tone unfriendly, her blue eyes firmly fixed on her man.

"Yes—no—" they both responded.

"We know each other from church," replied a smudge-faced Mary.

"Church! Did I hear correctly; you know each other from church?" Amy's incredulous eyes questioned; a stifled laugh escaping her red-lipsticked mouth. "Since when have you joined the God squad, Peter Brooke?" A hearty chuckle escaped her mouth, her brow arched in question and getting no immediate answers as Peter stood transfixed, his eyes and full attention on Mary.

He had lost all hope of ever seeing her again. And, here she was, as large as life and twice as beautiful in his eyes, even though her face was caked in motor oil and her hair askew; even though she paled into insignificance, when her looks were compared with the artificial and high-maintenance beauty of Amy Pilkington.

Peter's eyes dropped to the spanner clutched in Mary's hand, a smile dancing on his lips, his head shaking from side to side thinking, Goodness knows what she was thinking of doing with that. "What happened?" He asked.

After a brief account of the accident, Peter took the spanner from Mary's poised hand; closed the bonnet of the car, locked it and smiled indicating his car. "Hop in; sorry, I still don't know your name."

"Mary; my name is Mary Simpson."

"What do you mean, hop in, Peter; what on earth am I supposed to do, fly to the pub?" An icy-faced Amy enquired.

He smirked. "If you wish, dear, or you can sit in Mary's car and wait for me."

His eyes flitted to Mary. "You don't mind, do you?"

"No—no." She nodded her dishevelled head in agreement. "But—but your friend, will she…"

"She'll be ok," he sharply cut in, his eyes darting to Amy and clashing with eyes of pure venom. Turning his full attention on his new passenger he asked, "Where are you heading?"

"Home. I… I mean, the Sutton Estate, please," Mary's voice was subdued, her eyes flitting surreptitiously to a disgruntled woman throwing invisible daggers at both of them.

"No problem." He revved up the engine, his heart deflating. The Sutton Estate had a bad reputation and driving a top-notch gleaming sports car into that hell-hole did not thrill him at all.

Neither did the building they entered, as his shrewd eyes scanned the graffiti walls, the littered stairwell smelling of urine, the yobbo who roughly pushed past him; all a far cry from his plush five-bedroomed home on the other side of life. He sighed heavily ascending the grubby stairs, his feet coming to a stop outside a brown, paint-peeling door.

"You'd better go, Mister—Mister—"

"It's Peter Brooke."

She smiled gratefully and opened the door to the sound of gasping and sighing. Her urgent eyes turned to Peter, silently urging him to go, "Thank you; thank you, Mister Brooke."

He followed her in and what his eyes saw made his blood run cold. Fleeting uninvited thoughts of Amy evaporated into thin air as his eyes surveyed the grim surroundings, before following Mary to the source of the anguished moans and groans; his eyes lowering to the crumpled up heap on the floor. "Here, let me help." He slid his strong arms under the bundle and carried it to the bed, turning his bewildered eyes on Mary.

"My mother has multiple sclerosis," Mary replied before rushing off to her mother's side, tucking her into bed, replenishing her fresh water supply.

"Thank you, sir," the older woman replied, with a slight nod of her black and grey-black peppered head. "Thank you, sir," she repeated softly exuding a long, soft sigh.

He smiled his eyes surveying their miserable, cramped living conditions. Cramped, but everything in its right place, he assessed; everything clean, neat, tidy except—His eyes wandered to the smudge-faced, ruffled-haired Mary as a smile danced on his lips. "I think you better go and clean yourself up, Mary; I'll sit with your mother a while."

"But—but, Amy, your friend?"

"Go," insisted Peter, his eyes switching to the invalid.

"She's a good girl." Nodded the middle-aged woman; her voice a little stronger. "I don't know what I would have done without her since—since my Bertie's death earlier this year."

It all came crashing back into his mind as his eyes rested on the incapacitated woman in the bed. Bertie's funeral; his long-ago kind and helpful employer—Mary alone in the pew—at the graveside—The jigsaw started to assemble a picture in his head. Ten minutes later, Mary reappeared nicely scrubbed up, plumped up her mother's pillows and cast Peter a grateful smile. "Thank you for bringing me home, Mister Brooke." Feeling the colour rise to her cheeks, she averted her eyes, but not before his observant eyes noticed her shyness. He liked it; he liked it very much. It was, he thought, so very refreshing and he smiled. She did not notice his smile, aware only of the thousand fluttering butterflies dancing erratically in the pit of her stomach.

"You have a jewel, Missus Simpson, a rare jewel." He smiled at the bed-ridden lady, rose from her bed and approached the open door where Mary stood, silently urging him to disappear.

"Thank you," she managed to utter, her eyes firmly fixed on the flowered-patterned carpet below, her heart beating like the clappers.

"When can we have that coffee, Mary?" His eyes stared at her bent head, which he saw shake from side to side. "You owe me, Mary, for recovering you from your dismal fate."

Her subdued head rose, her blue eyes meeting the unflinching eyes of the man standing before her. "I am sorry, Mister Brooke; my mother needs me." She extended the door wider, willing him to go through, as a soft voice drifted towards the door.

"Your mother can cope perfectly well for an hour."

His eyes twinkled as he waited for Mary's reply, whilst the butterflies in her tummy now flew into her mind and became one mass of whirling confusion, making her heart tighten with sheer excitement at the prospect of an impending coffee date; her eyes closing as she mentally rummaged through her sparse wardrobe, wondering what she could wear and then—then—Amy crash-landed into her joyous world.

As if reading her thoughts, his astute eyes saw a glimpse of a shadow cross her eyes. "And, don't worry about Amy; she's just a casual friend."

She cast a sideway glance at her mother, who was beaming through her dilapidating illness and sighed resignedly. "Ok, coffee it is."

Two minds whirled that night in two opposite directions; one mind plotted, schemed and weaved an image of an easy lay; the other was full of nervous anxiety, searching for meaningful topics they could discuss.

His gleaming BMW came to a silent stop outside Mary's block of flats at precisely 15.50 p.m. and three confident, loud knocks were bestowed on the grubby-looking door at precisely 15.55 p.m. At precisely 15.56 p.m., Peter's eyes drank in a generous amount of disappointment as they stared at a young woman dressed in a plain, buttoned-up-to-the-neck white blouse and neat black skirt, finishing below the knees; her feet ensconced in a pair of sensible, low-heeled, black patent court shoes. He raised his eyes to her unblemished face, without a single trace of make-up, her blonde hair secured in her usual bun style. The term, *plain Jane*, in this case, plain Mary, came sharply into mind although, in reality, he hadn't been expecting much in terms of glamour; he was certainly expecting more than this.

Inwardly, she had shrivelled beneath his obvious disappointment that she could see in his eyes. She had, she dismally concluded, not passed the grade; she never did where fashion was concerned; for one, she did not have the money to splash out on expensive designer wear and, secondly, if she did have the money she would no sooner waste it on the here today, gone tomorrow fashion trend, then she would on a rock concert. Her eyes, however, appreciated what she saw before her; a neatly attired, well-groomed, shiny-shoed gentleman standing on her doorstep. However, the little confidence she had was fast disappearing; any grains she had mustered made her shrink beneath his gaze. She yearned to run— run—run—anywhere would do, so long as she was not within a two-kilometre radius of this self-assured, self-possessed, over-confident specimen of a man. She stood glued to the spot, unable to move a centimetre, her heart palpitating furiously, while her guts twisted and turned, her eyes unwillingly focused on the man standing before her.

Without warning he brushed past her and approached Missus Simpson's bed and, from behind his back, produced the biggest bouquet of mixed roses the woman had ever seen, making her eyes stretch and simultaneously sparkle and her heart warm towards this rare visitor. He turned his attention away from the invalid. "For you." He handed Mary a small bunch of sweet peas and, in that split second, the young woman's estimation of him grew ten-fold, giving rise to a small smile playing on her lips. Perhaps he wasn't quite the egoistical guy she had made him out to be.

"Thank you." Her smile widened, as her trembling hands took the fragrant flowers. "Thank you very much, Peter."

He watched as she raised the sweet peas up to her face and inhaled deeply their sweet fragrance, closing her eyes in innocent pleasure, as his thoughts diverted to his many exes and his mind questioned if any of them would have been satisfied with such a mere gesture.

Her eyes dropped to the large slab of coffee and walnut gateau before flitting to Peter. "I shall never get into my clothes if…" Her sentence remained incomplete as her eyes met his, feeling the profusion of colour rising to her face. Her eyes dropped, fingers nervously clutching a teaspoon as she stirred her coffee round and round—round and round not daring, even for a split second, to glance at him again. She felt the warm touch of his broad hand over her free hand, as she silently confounded her nerves.

Like an uncontrollable electrical current, both felt the stark tension of opposites charge through their consciousness, silently driving a wedge between them but, at the same time, like two magnets, attracting their opposites together, until the heavy shroud of doom overpowered her making her admonish herself severely. It can never be, she closed her eyes tightly. Their worlds were too far removed, her social status crashed into her dismal thoughts and, without lifting her eyes from her cup, she said softly, "Thank you, Peter, for the coffee and gateau."

His quizzical eyes shot to her, his brow furrowing in playful amusement. "Actually, Mary, aren't you the one treating me?"

A renewed wave of crimson rose to her cheeks, suffusing her whole body in a deep shade of embarrassment. "I…erm…yes, y…yes, of course," she stammered, her eyes dropping to her handbag, where her trembling fingers searched frantically for her purse; deeper and deeper they plunged, wishing she could go there with them; more fervently they searched, her eyes stuck in her bag, her brow creasing into puzzled lines; a slight, but audible, tremor in her words of confession. "I seem to have forgotten my purse." Her eyes shot to his eyes of twinkling amusement, lowering to the mischievous smile dancing on his lips.

Suddenly his smile died a sudden death and vanished, his eyes losing their playful gloss and growing icy cold, his voice matching his eyes. "Then, Miss

Simpson, there is only one thing for it." His disciplined eyes surveyed the noticeable anxiety seeping into her eyes, her still-set face, her brow furrowed in worry. "You will take me out to dinner."

His deadly serious eyes seemed to drill into the depths of her very soul, her will to live hastily evaporating and her earlier assessment of the man she was looking at rapidly changing, as she silently cursed herself for her forgetfulness. How could she have been so utterly stupid? She asked herself over and over again, as she felt herself crumble beneath his powerful gaze. And, how could she possibly afford to fund two restaurant meals? She could hardly afford to pay the bills. "I'll send the money for the coffee and gateau to you," she volunteered, her ears attuned to his words, her eyes on his stone-cold face.

"Dinner. Tomorrow at eight o'clock sharp; you owe me, Miss Simpson."

"But...but..."

"No *buts*, Miss Simpson; tomorrow, eight o'clock sharp."

His eyes followed her into the run-down block of flats, as he sat behind the wheel of his plush BMW. She was, he thought, like a timid rabbit, trespassing in unfamiliar territory; probably still a virgin; perhaps, she'd never ever had a steady boyfriend. So, what the heck was he doing sitting outside her block, staring after this inexperienced woman, when he could have his fill of experienced females and, there was always Amy he could run back to; what the hell was he doing here, when he could click his fingers and have a beauty at his side in no time at all? The lids of his eyes closed on a disappearing Mary and he sat back, the soft leather upholstery perfectly moulding with the contours of his back. What was it about Mary Simpson that was so damned appealing? The answer immediately crashed into his head. It was the uniqueness of Mary Simpson; pure and simple.

He would, he calculated, need to tread very carefully; the last thing he wanted was to scare her off. There were three important things to consider: her obvious inexperience of men; her devotion to her mother and her faith; three facts which were to him completely alien; his sexual experience was second to none; the only faith he had was in money and status and as for his mother—he felt a sharp-pointed blade slice through his heart. Snapping out of his reverie he sat up, turned on the ignition and sped out of the Sutton Estate.

The empty winding roads gave him no solace as distorted images of his mother flitted in and out of his head and, as always, he pushed them to the back of his mind, pulled up at the nearest pub and ordered himself a double, neat vodka.

Meals at exclusive restaurants were interspersed with casual drinks in quaint local country pubs, lattes at the small, popular coffee shop, the odd evening out at the cinema and a day out at the beach, Missus Simpson accompanying them on the latter excursion. Their friendship grew. Hopes for anything further to develop struggled to rise to the surface. On one occasion, Peter cautiously asked Mary about her exes, watched her visibly pale and her mouth remaining obstinately shut.

In bed, he lay staring at the stark ceiling above, wondering what kind of idiot he was pursuing a girl who, to the outside world, was a timid mouse, a religious freak and someone who, seemingly, had never had a sexual experience in her life. "I must be stark raving mad," he said aloud over and over again and there and then he made a plan; either he was going to bed her or he was going to get rid of her; he had no doubt that their current casual, platonic friendship would end up being the inevitable fallout.

She lay in her bed, her ears attuned to her mother's coughing and wheezing in the next room, as thoughts of Peter filtered into her mind and dissolved all other thoughts; a smile spreading on to her face as a warm, cosy, secure feeling, like a comforting blanket, wrapped itself around her. Despite his glamorous image and his self-assured mannerisms, she thought, there was something genuinely nice about him; she also knew he had been deeply hurt, maybe even damaged; her sensitive eyes had seen it in his faraway look. There was, she had concluded, a mystery shrouding this man.

As they sat in the restaurant, both had different agendas spinning in their minds; his agenda was to get to know Mary Simpson sexually; her agenda was to delve into his emotional background where, hopefully, she would find some answers. Catching his intense eyes on her she queried, "What is it, Peter?"

His unwavering gaze lingered on her. "I was going to ask you the same thing; tell me about your former boyfriends, Mary."

Like a wild tsunami, a surge of inexplicable resentment invaded and washed through her, making her narrowed eyes viciously shoot up to him, "What business is it of yours?"

Eyes locked with eyes, both looking into each other's souls and seeing only a void, an emptiness; a dark hollow where deep, personal, secret emotions lay undisturbed, until now.

The echo of her raw, cold words reverberated in his head. "I just wondered," he said with an expression.

"It's none of your business," she reiterated her eyes dropping to the crisp, starched, white tablecloth as she felt her whole timid-self retreating into her protective shell, as a heavy silence obliterated the sounds around them and shrouded them and their thoughts. Seconds, impregnated with tension, ticked away until finally they were punctured. "I had one boyfriend; we were actually childhood sweethearts and ended up being engaged. He was killed in a car crash." She threw the staccato-like words out of her reluctant mouth, her eyes glued to the tablecloth, while his shocked and regretful eyes shot to her pale face.

"I am sorry," he said softly his words laden with meaning, as a glimpse of her life seeped into his well of regret.

Her eyes darted to him. "And you; your exes?" She asked.

"No one important." His eyes met her questioning eyes. "I haven't met the right one."

"And Amy?"

He smiled shaking his head in silence.

Rising abruptly she threw her napkin on to the table. "I need to get back to Mum; she'll be needing me," she stated avoiding his eyes.

They travelled in silence, wrapped in each other's revelations, intermingled with the soft purring of the car's engine, until they reached their destination and all became silent.

"Thank you," she said as she turned to locate the door handle and felt his strong, broad hands on her arms turning her towards him. Reluctantly, she turned and felt his warm lips on her mouth; at first soft and lingering and then his mouth becoming possessive and passionate, as she felt her whole body surrendering and yielding under his hypnotic spell. *Stop him.* Her fuzzy head commanded. Ignoring her head's sense of logic, she allowed herself to be mesmerised further by his passion; allowing her stifled emotions to surge and fuse together, mixing into a potent recipe of desire, want and need as she passionately kissed him back.

"Stop!" She demanded as if she was suddenly doused with petrol and ignited, the hot burning flames in her eyes linking with pure desire in his eyes. She felt his hands releasing her arms, a heavy wave of disappointment washing over her. I didn't mean it, she yearned to cry out. *Hold me; kiss me again; I didn't mean it—I didn't mean it—*

"Sorry," his word sliced through her heart as she repeatedly cursed her inhibitions; her rules of conduct; her feelings of betrayal.

The click of the car door resounded in his ears, as he watched her disappear into the confines of her sanctuary, his lips curling into a satisfied smile. It would take time, but he would achieve his goal; her response to his kiss confirmed it. He would give her time and, in the meantime, he had Amy.

His phone calls and messages went unheeded and unanswered; his flowers and cards returned by the next post; his fervent knocks on her door were ignored leaving him with his only option; to persevere more zealously and, finally, his tenacity paid dividends but, not in the way he expected.

The door opened to a glassy, red-eyed young woman whose face was pale and drawn; whose demeanour indicated sadness, despondency and resignation. "Please go," were the only two words she volunteered, as she immediately proceeded to close the door on her uninvited and unwanted caller.

"Mary…please tell me, what on earth is the matter?" Peter asked, his own words tinged with uncharacteristic anxiety for, clearly, there was something terribly wrong.

Her tear-stained eyes focused on the man standing before her. "It's Mum; she's in hospital. It's…it's serious."

"Let me in, Mary."

She extended the door, any fight in her long gone.

His eyes scanned the small room and rested on Missus Simpson's neatly made bed, his ears attuned to the fresh surge of uncontrollable sobbing escaping from Mary. Instantly, he was by her side his strong, comforting arms around her slender body as he brought her closer to himself, soothing her with his sympathetic words, while she rested in his strong embrace and felt an inexplicable peace wash over her and enter her soul; her eyes momentarily closed to this world and its pain, feeling only his warmth and the reassurance of his toned body next to hers; his arms around her as if he was temporarily shielding her from the darkness and pain that was inevitably to come.

She would have been happy to stay in this secure bubble forever, if it wasn't for the chiming of the clock, bringing her back to the stark, brutal reality and the pain it brought. "It's…it's her heart." She managed to extract the words in between intermittent, heavy bouts of sobbing. "Her heart is giving up. She's going to d…die." A fresh attack of grief overtook her, making her whole body wrench and heave before it, once more, surrendered to two comforting arms, her mind oblivious to his soothing words; already planning the hymns for her mother's funeral.

He stayed with her throughout the following days moving in, sleeping on the lumpy sofa; making meals and tidying the small flat, while Mary spent every last second she could with her mother and when the inevitable came, he was her rock, her fortress and her solace.

After the burial, he returned to his own sumptuous home, sat alone at one end of the elegant Italian polished table and reflected. Everything had changed regarding Mary. No longer did he wish to have mere sex with her and then dispense of her like an old sock. She was worth more than that; far, far more. She was, he concluded, a rare jewel to be treated with the utmost respect. She was not a sex object. She was a woman; a damaged woman. Death had seen to that; death of her fiancé; death of her father; death of her mother and now the grief had to be dealt with appropriately.

Mary Simpson, he concluded, needed time to reflect, to grieve, to learn how to smile, to learn how to be happy again and only time, precious time, could come to her assistance. It could take a month, a year, or five years, but he determined, he would be there for her; her kiss had told him it was not over. Now he would have to support her as a friend, a confidante and one day, he hoped, as a lover.

Peter Brooke

His innocent eyes looked up at her as they walked hand-in-hand down the long, straight road; his mouth breaking out into a wide, content smile. She was his world.

As she looked down on him she smiled, the dimples in his cheeks making her heart tug. He was everything to her.

Mother and son; son and mother; an unbreakable unit into which no one could barge or damage; or, so they thought.

Two days after Emily Brooke had given birth to her one and only child, her husband had walked out the door and out of their lives and mother and son never saw him again.

As Ralph Brooke walked out, other things entered and one of them was Emily's deep mistrust of men, for Ralph had been everything she had found admirable in a man; he was kind, honest, hard-working and caring; a pillar of the local community and if he had simply walked out, there was no hope for anyone else. And so, she took on the arduous role of looking after her son on her own; fervently promising him that she would be mother and father to him; that she would never, ever let him down.

Peter, now eight years of age, walked hand-in-hand with his mum, he thought, he was the luckiest boy on the planet; feeling immensely proud to be her son and happy that she had so many friends to talk to at the school gate but, there was one little thing niggling him and, taking a little breath, he decided now would be the best time to ask. "Mummy," he looked up to her, "who is that man who keeps smiling at you?"

She dropped her eyes and smiled, "What man, cherub?"

"The man who always smiles at you; look…look, he's there." He pointed his little chubby finger straight ahead.

"Oh…ah; I don't really know who he is. I guess his child goes to your school."

"Who?"

"I really don't know, Son."

They walked on, drawing nearer to the mixed crowd of children and grown-ups mingling around the gates. "He's smiling at you, Mummy."

A host of unruly butterflies flitted around in the pit of Emily's stomach. She knew it was absolutely absurd; after all, he was a stranger who, on occasion, nodded and smiled her way but, nevertheless, the wild butterflies were erratically dancing a merry dance, as her feet approached the crowded gates and her eyes caught his friendly smile.

Impulsively, the young boy tugged at his mother's coat sleeve and pulled her forward towards the smiling man. "Hello," chirped Peter, his young eyes looking up at the chubby face, with a crop of mousy hair resting across his forehead in an uneven fringe. "My mummy wants to know your name." Whereupon the colour drained from Emily's shocked face and the butterflies in her stomach transformed into heavy-footed elephants, churning her stomach into a tight knot of embarrassment, reaching up to her brain and killing all words of denial.

"Malcolm; my name is Malcolm and who may you be, little fellow?" His smiling eyes rested on Peter, making him instantly feel very grand and important.

"My name is Peter." He extended his chubby hand.

Malcolm shook his hand and extended it to Emily.

"And my mummy's name is, Mummy," piped Peter.

"Hello, Mummy," Malcolm smiled at Emily, turned to the young boy and winked, making Peter smile from ear to ear.

"I am Emily." Emily begrudgingly extended her hand, thinking how she was going to reprimand her son for his straightforwardness.

Their friendship grew. Mother and son were happy in their mutual knowledge that they had found a new friend. For weeks, they just talked at the school gates and got on with their respective lives until, one afternoon, Peter ran out of the school building towards them at full speed, planted a three-dimensional rocket into his mother's hands and tugged Malcolm's hand. "Why don't you come home with us and have some tea?"

"Peter," Emily's shocked eyes darted to her son, then flitted to Malcolm. "I'm sorry, Peter should not have said that. Please accept my apo…"

"I'd love to come, Peter," Malcolm conspiratorially smiled at the young boy, before raising expectant eyes, only to witness a deep flush of red rapidly infusing Emily's cheeks, making his smile widen.

By now, the young boy had switched his tugging allegiance and was furiously pulling his mother's hand. "Please…please, Mummy; please let

Malcolm come to tea; pl…ee…ee…se. He can play rockets with me…please, Mummy."

Feelings of mixed frustration, anger, annoyance, excitement and humiliation bubbled and surged through Emily's fast-pulsating veins. If she had the nerve to admonish her son there and then, she would have surely done so. Instead, she found herself involuntarily nodding her head and mumbling, "Ok."

"When…when…when…when…when?" Peter, like an out-of-control jumping bean, jumped up and down, his happy eyes flitting from one adult to the other in constant succession.

"Tomorrow, after school," she heard the echo of her reluctant words coming out of her mouth; furiously, hoping against hope, that Malcolm would be intelligent enough to know she had been put on the spot and decline the reluctant invitation.

"I can't wait." He beamed at the young, happy boy.

And, while one young heart soared; another sank to the depths of inner despair.

She looked down on her son as they walked home alone, her inner fury dissipating with each step but, not enough to stop her asking, "Why did you invite Malcolm to tea, Peter?"

She felt his hand break free from her hand as he ran forward, stopped and glanced back. "Because…because he's a nice…nice man."

She smiled and began to make plans.

That night sleep eluded her. In its place, images of Ralph and Malcolm wove and interwove, linked and interlinked, mingled and intermingled until it all became a blurry whirly mass. Roughly throwing her bedcover aside, she put on her robe, peered into Peter's room and made herself a mug of cocoa. Sitting at the table, her cold hands wrapped around her hot mug, her mind drifted to a time long ago, before Peter was born; to a time when she had found happiness and thought it would be her's forever. How fragile, she now thought, that happiness was. One minute Ralph, strong and reliant, was in her life; her everything, and the next minute, he was gone without a word and without trace though; after a year after his departure, she had heard that he'd gone to America. Never once did she think of pursuing him; if he'd disappeared, he'd disappeared for a reason; end of story. Since Ralph there had been men who had been interested; she had turned her attention away from all of them. And now—now this Malcolm chap was arriving for tea. She shook her head dismally from side to side; she needed him to come to tea, as much as she needed a hole in the head.

And, why Peter had asked him over was beyond her comprehension. A sudden thought crashed into her head, making instant lines appear on her brow. Unless—unless he wanted some sort of father figure. Rising she popped her empty mug into the sink and snapping the light off she muttered as she marched up the stairs, "I'll have to nip that idea well and truly out of his little head."

The doorbell rang. One heart leapt; the other sank. Peter preceded his mother to the door and, jumping excitedly from foot to foot, waited for her to open it. "We've got sausage rolls, chicken and salad sandwiches and other things and…and ice cream for afters!" He exclaimed as the door opened.

"Wow; my favourite things," Malcolm chuckled, presenting a small bunch of freesias to Emily and a large bag of assorted sweets for Peter, making the young boy's eyes shine with sheer happiness.

Her guts churned and her heart full of dread, Emily wished it was the end of the ordeal. Sighing deeply, surreptitious eyes darted to the clock on the wall. She had at least half an hour of excruciating torture to bear. "Come in," she said, though not as enthusiastically as Malcolm had hoped, for he had tried to catch Emily's eye for weeks.

Two people sat at opposite sides of the table, while Peter sat next to his mother and jabbered on about school, his friends, football; his extensive marble collection and his favourite comic. One adult hoped the other would make his polite excuses and leave, knowing that she had invited him here under duress; the other adult searched for appropriate words to ask his host out on a proper date, without the infuriating son in tow; although, he was quick to realise, this infuriating son could be instrumental in actually securing a date. He cast a smile in Peter's direction. "Tell me about your favourite superhero, young man."

Ten minutes later, Peter ran out of *Wow* words to describe the man who drove around in a bat mobile with his special friend, Robin, saving people from all kinds of dismal fates; ran up the stairs to his bedroom, grabbed his favourite book about his superhero and charged back down the stairs, to show his book to his new friend, while Malcolm seized his chance without Peter's assistance, "How about a coffee sometime, Emily?"

She rose. "I'll pop the kettle on."

"I mean, you and I; perhaps somewhere in town when Peter is in school."

The look of incredulity thrown his way did not stir him; her next words did. "What about your child…children?"

His mind whirled erratically, his eyes unintentionally staring at the woman now standing before him. Did she know and, if she did know, what did she know? "My…erm…children?" He heard the booming echo of his own words.

"The one, or ones, you take and pick up from the school," she interrupted his whirling thoughts.

His fast-pumping heart decreased its rapid beating, as a surge of relief washed over him. She didn't know; it was an innocent question and the truthful answer came out of his dry mouth. "Oh, I have no children at school, Emily. I pick up my sister's daughter. My sister is a single parent and relies heavily on my help."

His words immediately created the desired impact of Emily seeing him as the person he wished to portray; a caring, respectable man who was looking out for his sister and his niece. Words rushed out of her mouth before she could stop them. "I'd love a coffee date." And, before the last word escaped her mouth, she felt like screaming at the top of her voice at her own damned impetuousness.

"Are you going out on a date with Malcolm, Mummy?" Peter enquired his eyes flitting from his mother to Malcolm and back to his mother, his hands clutching tightly his superhero book.

"Little ears," chuckled Emily and all three laughed.

An array of plain and sparkling attire of all colours flew out of the wardrobe: skirts, tops and dresses of all styles and lengths, followed by an assortment of shoes and sandals, rapidly cluttering Emily's normally pristine bedroom. She sat down amidst the chaos, utterly exhausted, forlorn and fed up as she stared at her reflection in the full-length cheval mirror. I must be stark raving mad, she told herself, to have ever considered, let alone agreed, to a date with a man I barely know. Shaking her head in incredulity, she picked up a black sequined cocktail dress and assessed its potentiality. "I am going for a simple coffee date, not a lavish banquet, for goodness sake." She admonished herself severely, her eyes lingering on the expensive dress, the only designer item she owned, as memories crashed into her head… *It had been such a happy occasion; a fifth wedding anniversary and, oh, how they had danced! And, how they had made ecstatic love that night…*

It was the first and the last time she had worn the dress, soon after she had learned that she was pregnant. "Where are you, Ralph?" She whispered softly, her eyes staring into oblivion; suddenly blinking back into reality, as the door downstairs banged and thudding feet pounded up the stairs, the sound of her son's excited voice ringing loud and clear in her ears as he proudly announced, "I scored a goal, Mum!" and she felt the tight tug her heart, as her lips broke out into a smile. Peter was growing up fast; already the apron strings were loosening. He had his own group of friends, played his own games; dreamed his own dreams. The smile died on her lips. Soon, she would just simply be his mum; an essential partner for his chess game, but no longer a reader of bedtime stories; not a pirate in his divertissements but simply good, old mum. He would take care of himself but not yet—not yet.

Guilt stabbed at her heart. "Are you sure you don't mind me going for a coffee with Malcolm, Peter?" She held both his arms in her hands, her eyes looking deep into his hoping he would say, *Yes, I do mind, Mummy; I don't want you to go out with that Malcolm man. I want you to stay at home with me.* Instead, his exuberant words cut her in two.

"I like Malcolm; he's nice, Mummy. I want you to have a coffee with him." His words put a seal on any second thoughts she had; her eyes following his disappearing figure as he dashed out of the room and into his own bedroom, to secretly tell his superhero about his news.

Exuding a deep sigh, Emily picked up a pair of smart beige trousers and a white blouse and placed them carefully over a chair, ready for her date with Malcolm.

The three loud knocks on the door, made her eyes shoot to the carriage clock on the mantelpiece. One o'clock precisely; it was him! Grabbing her shoulder bag, she stepped into her low-heeled shoes and approached the door; her insides churning mercilessly, her heart palpitating rapidly, forcing a smile onto her face as she placed her trembling fingers on the handle and opened the door; her astounded eyes widening as she spotted a gleaming, white Mercedes on the roadside; her heart swiftly plummeting as a pretentious, egotistical, over-confident, pompous man was the last thing she wanted in her life. And, here he stood and here she was glaring at the motor, as if her eyes were stuck to the machine with super-glue.

"You like?" He winked, making her guts turn ice-cold.

How could she stand there and tell him she abhorred it and everything it represented? Begrudgingly, she nodded her head.

"Good, I do too." He opened the passenger door and she slid inside, but not before her nostrils caught a whiff of lingering, sensual perfume, making her stomach wrench and her mind wander.

He switched on the ignition; the coolness and softness of the subtle leather upholstery, immediately created in her a soothing effect and, in seconds, her mind was in tune with the soft, relaxing purring sound of the engine. Her eyes followed his chubby fingers as he slipped in a CD and the tranquil sounds of Chopin's Nocturne started to cast its soothing magic, making her eyes close. She snapped them open. Peter! Her eyes closed once more. He had given her his permission; after all, he was practically the one who had initiated the coffee date. And, yes, she firmly told herself, that's all it was, a coffee date; half an hour in a coffee bar as a mark of friendship; that was all. And then, she could say *goodbye* and *good riddance* to this pretentious specimen of a man, his gleaming motor and all that they both symbolised.

The half-hour turned into an hour and yet, it seemed to Emily, that barely twenty minutes had passed as she listened, chatted and laughed in Malcolm's engaging company; her first impressions of him swiftly readjusting, leaving her to conclude that it was his flashy car that was ostentatious; Malcolm, himself, seemed rather down-to-earth, casual, friendly; interested in her and, more importantly, in Peter; the latter trait being a big plus in his favour. A dark thought crashed into her mind. "You're not married are you, Malcolm?" His loud chuckle told her he was not. "And children?" She raised a questioning eyebrow, for she knew the two sometimes did not go together.

"Temporarily, I look out for Claire's daughter, my niece." He smiled.

On their next date, they were accompanied by Peter and loads of animals and, after they had spent a fun-packed day at the zoo, Peter gave Malcolm his full approval, giving him the green light to become a fixture in his and his mother's life and once again laughter rang out in the Brooke household and new dreams were made.

Emily and Peter's lives changed dramatically. They moved out of their compact semi-detached and into a six-bedroomed house and rapidly their friends and attitudes changed too. The two-some became a three-some and all decisions big, small and anything in between were mutually made; they became a close-knit unit.

As with all chains, there is always a weak link and the weak link was Peter, not because he was the youngest, but because he was the strongest; the one who ultimately formed the decisions for, unbeknown to him, it was he who held his mother's key; to turn or not to turn and, if to turn, which way.

Malcolm was well aware that everything lay in the young boy's hands; he knew children well; he understood well the mother-child bond and he was well versed in the finer details of the game because he had played it numerous times. This, he had told himself after his first encounter with Peter, was no different. He would have to gain the young boy's trust and only then could he begin to weave his plan, to get the sprog out of the way and have Emily for himself; then, when he had finished with her, she could have her precious son back and he would move on to his next victim.

Emily looked out of the large, panoramic kitchen widow, her happy eyes surveying the sprawling, well-manicured garden and smiled. Never had she been so content than at this point in her life. Her eyes followed her son and his guardian as they planted bulbs together, watered their treasures and planted some more, before engaging in a kick-around with Peter's new football. Her heart sliced in two. This, she concluded, is what Peter needed all along; a father figure, a male role model he could look up to, respect and emulate. She closed her eyes on the heart-warming scene; satisfied. Her eyes popped open at the wild screams of pure delight. Peter had scored a goal and, while she pondered on all her blessings, little did she know that, while the man and her boy were playing football, seeds of doubt, like the recently planted bulbs, were beginning to grow in her subconscious mind.

The seeds of doubt were hidden, for it was not their time to grow, mature, or yield; their time was not yet but it would surely come, just as night follows day and thunder follows lightning and, in the meantime, the seeds were carefully overseen and nurtured by an expert.

Tea time was a special time when the three of them would bond together; laying the table with a starched, crisp, white tablecloth and sparkling crockery; making the meal together; sitting down at the table together and catching up on each other's news. It was a very special time for the seeds of doubt to thrive.

Heartily, Peter tucked into his spaghetti Bolognese. "This is absolutely yummy, Mummy!" He exclaimed shoving into his mouth another forkful, whilst proceeding to give a full and detailed account, of how Miss Harley had happened to find a live spider in her desk drawer.

The clash of metal against porcelain made two pairs of eyes simultaneously dart to Malcolm. "Peter, do not talk with your mouth full of food," he stated as a sharp, pointed lance pierced through Emily's pained heart, her unblinking eyes set on Malcolm, for it was not what he had said but his cold, detached words, without a trace of inflexion, which hurt. Detaching herself from his stern gaze she turned her attention to her son. "Peter, you know, you must not talk when you have food in your mouth."

"Sorry," he said looking sheepish, gulped down his last mouthful of spaghetti, touched with a mixed sauce of minced beef, onion and tomato, rose from his chair and turned away.

"Peter, sit," Malcolm's no-nonsense eyes rose to the retreating child.

A second thrust, this time sharper and deeper, plunged into Emily's heart, her ears attuned to the echo of her own detached words. "We are not quite finished yet, Peter. Just sit down and wait a while."

Peter's innocent eyes flitted from one adult to another and back to his mother. Were they playing a silly grown-up game, he wondered, lowering his eyes onto his empty plate, whilst trying desperately to control his burning urge to burp.

Vigorously rubbing the cream into her hands, Emily threw a disconcerted look at her husband. "What was all that about at the table, Malcolm?"

He peered over the cover of his thick thriller tome. "The boy needs to learn some manners, Emily," he stated before readjusting his eyes back onto the page.

"He just wanted to share his news about his day," she counteracted swiftly.

Without raising his eyes off the page he reinstated, "The boy needs to learn manners; he'll never get anywhere in the world without them."

She climbed into bed and turned her back on him.

The seed had begun to grow.

Two pairs of eyes looked directly at the middle-aged woman sitting before them, her smile reassuring. "Please don't worry, Peter is doing well but, I feel, he could do far better if he only applied himself more," Peter's teacher stated firmly, making Emily's heart plummet into a well of silent despair, for this was the third time she had heard the familiar words; not to mention Malcolm's constant reiteration that Peter could do a hell of a lot better.

Side by side they sat; the air in the car heavy and still around them, the soft purring of the engine the only sound audible. Finally, Malcolm's damning, measured words sliced through the heavy atmosphere. "Something has got to be done about Peter, Emily."

Her eyes shot to him. "What do you mean, Malcolm?"

Staring directly ahead, his hands firmly around the wheel, in control of the car and the woman inside, he stated in clear, concise words, "I mean, Peter is an intelligent boy; this…this school of his is doing him no justice. The boy needs a strict regime before it is too late, Emily."

Her fast-beating heart turned to stone, her blood into a sheet of ice, while her mind raced incessantly. Forcibly she expunged the words from her mouth. "What exactly do you mean, Malcolm?"

"I mean, we need to withdraw him from this mediocre school; we need to find him a first-class educational establishment and, don't worry about the cost, I'll cover it."

Her thumping heart stopped, her stark eyes glared ahead into the solace of the gathering dusk, her words as cold and stark as her eyes. "You mean, send him away?"

His fingers clenched tighter the wheel, making his knuckles visibly protrude. He'd been through this rigmarole before; he knew how to choose his words carefully. "Yes, purely for the sake of his education. Peter needs the best; don't you think the same, Emily?"

"The best your money can buy," she said her words cold, detached, leaving lingering echoes on her moving lips.

He bit back the words that sprang to his mind; he had to tread carefully if he was to get his way, he told himself. His eyes intermittent between his partner and the road ahead, he continued on his mission. "I mean, Emily, the best money can provide for your son." He let his words sink in before he added, "Don't you want the very best for your son, Emily?"

Her firmly set mouth, eyes staring directly ahead, the silence and iciness she exuded told him everything he needed to know. He would have to up his game; shroud it with subtle persuasion and work on breaking the mother-son bond; the sooner, the better.

The ritualistic making of the evening meal and laying the table continued in the same mode, with one exception; casual conversation had transformed into acts of courtesy between the adults while Peter, oblivious to the heavy atmosphere, continued to chatter enthusiastically, causing pain and annoyance in equal measures; causing his mother's heart to sear into a thousand excruciating pieces, as she dared to contemplate a single day without the presence of her son; causing Malcolm's blood to boil, with a mixture of impatience and irritation at the boy's incessant chatter.

They sat in their usual places and before them, two plates of untouched shepherd's pie and one empty plate apart from one solitary golden chip, which was quickly scooped up onto a fork and stuffed into Peter's waiting mouth. "Can I go out to play now, Mummy?" He rose from the chair.

Malcolm took his chance, denying his partner to answer her son, his solemn eyes staring fixedly at the boy. "Peter, we need to talk."

Peter's innocent eyes looked up to the eyes he trusted and saw his guardian's serious face; his young eyes dropping to Malcolm's stern-set mouth. Had he done something naughty? He searched his head, his feet itching to join his friend, Billy, as he hopped about impatiently, thinking of the tadpoles they'd catch in their respective jars. Reluctantly, Peter sat back down his, big, sullen, green eyes focused on the man sitting directly opposite him; willing him to hurry and say what he had to say; tadpoles were waiting.

"Not now, Malcolm." He heard his mother's soft pleading voice, his eyes following her hand, as she extended it across the table and placed it lightly on her partner's hand, her begging eyes hoping for some sort of clemency; Peter neither understood nor was in the slightest bit bothered about. It was, after all, grown-up stuff and he was far more interested in how many wriggly specimens he was soon going to catch and bring back home to his mum.

"Now!" insisted Malcolm his strong voice firm, detached, decisive, authoritarian; his cold eyes refusing to meet those of the woman sitting opposite him.

Emily released her hand from the touch of Malcolm's cold skin, lowering her dejected eyes to the mound on her plate, consisting of minced beef topped with golden mashed potato. How utterly unappetising it all looked, she thought, closing her eyes to it all; her ears finely attuned to Malcolm rising, stepping away from the table, water gurgling into a glass and foreboding footsteps coming nearer—nearer.

His cough, a preamble to his words; the words which would inevitably send her precious son away, sent sparks of icy sharp shivers up and down her spine, making her fervently wish she had never met this man, let alone agree to move in with him and yet—yet—she loved him with all of her heart, body, mind and soul.

Peter shifted in his chair. The tadpoles were waiting for him.

"Peter."

The solitary word sent a sharp-pointed blade through Emily's already broken heart. "Peter, your mum and I need to have a very important chat with you," Malcolm's tone was soft but firm.

It can't be as important as the tadpoles, thought the young boy. Slowly he raised his eyes to his guardian. The quicker this was over and done with; the quicker he could go.

Emily squeezed her eyes tightly, her silent words going round and round in her head... *I do not want any of this. This...this is not my doing; this...this is not my doing...not my doing...not my doing...* She squeezed her eyes harder blocking everything and everyone out.

"We have found a fantastic school for you, Peter; a school you will do very well in; a school you will be very happy at."

Peter's shocked eyes shot and bore into hard, steely eyes. "But, I'm happy at Saint Bartholomews; I don't want to go to another school; I've got lots and lots and lots and...lots of friends at my school." His glassy-sheened eyes remained firmly fixed on Malcolm, who exuded a preliminary cough, before continuing with his well-rehearsed explanation of the matter, while Emily's heart crashed and burned.

Peter listened attentively; he had no option if he wanted to join his friend. Slowly, his interest awoke and gathered momentum and the more he listened, the more his heart was warmed to the subject and the more Emily's heart tore into broken shards of undiluted pain.

"And so you see, young Peter, not only will you get a fabulous education; you'll be engaged in lots of sporting activities I know, for a fact, you love. And, friends, well, you'll have more than you could possibly wish to have."

"What about Billy Moffatt?"

"You'll see Billy when you come home for a visit."

Peter's eyes flitted to his mother, who was sitting motionless like a sitting statue. She had already started the grieving process. "Mummy will miss me." His innocent eyes switched to Malcolm; his words cut a wedge out of Emily's raw heart, her watery eyes turning to her son as she pinned on a watery smile; her guts twisting treacherously, as if they were mercilessly twisting the very life out of her, forcing words out of her dry mouth. "I'll be all right, Son, as long as this is what you want."

He nodded his head.

"Is it what you want?" Her words were laden with a mixture of heavy foreboding, unnerving misgivings and concern. "Is it really what you want, Peter?" Her solemn eyes went deep into his very soul.

"Yep," he chirped. "Can I go now?"

"Enjoy your tad-poling, Peter," enthused Malcolm, as a heavy surge of relief surged through his entire body. It had been much easier than he thought it would have been. The *click* of the door was followed, some seconds later, by a second *click* of the outside door, leaving Malcolm to revel in his successful achievement.

She placed one heavy foot in front of the other, bitter salt tears streaming down her face; her heart empty, except for the sheer excruciating pain of loss punctuated by the *stab-stab-stab* of Malcolm's invisible but oh so palpable dagger—*stab-stab-stab-stab-stab-stab-stab-stab.* Her feet came to a sudden halt, her eyes peering through the glass. There were bottles, many bottles, stacked on the shelves and jostling for attention. Swiping away the remnant of tears on her dampened face, she stared unblinkingly at the clear, brown, green coloured bottles; larger ones, smaller ones, miniatures; square shaped ones, even oval-shaped flagons with eye-catching, crystal-like tops. Gingerly she pushed the glass door open, to the delightful tinkling sound of a bell, walked inside and approached the counter. "Something strong, please," her voice trembled and her eyes rested firmly on the counter, for fear of what the licensee should think.

"Oh, Missus Brooke, I'm sorry, I didn't recognise you; I apologise; what is it you wanted?"

Emily squeezed her eyes tightly yearning to run, hide, to obliterate everybody and everything from her mind. She turned.

"Missus Brooke, it's Joyce; Joyce Cummings, your old neighbour."

Emily craved to crawl into the biggest, deepest, darkest pit; shrivel up and die. Involuntarily, her eyes looked up and their eyes briefly locked, as Emily willed her lips to form into a smile. "Hello, Joyce. Something strong please; we're having a party and, astonishingly, running low; something strong please," she repeated, knowing how ridiculously feeble and stupid her obvious lie sounded.

"Coming up," Joyce hastened to oblige her former neighbour. "How is Malcolm?" She asked hesitantly, before placing the bottle on the scuffed counter.

"He's good," Emily forced the words out, yearning to scream at the top of her voice…*he's a betrayer; he's evil…evil…evil…*aching to run out of the small shop and into the alluring dark, deep hole, she'd already dug in her mind's-eye, as she furiously dug her fingers into the depths of her deep pockets, her heart sinking in despair, as her wistful eyes stared down at the clear liquid in the tall bottle and her fingers brought out nothing. "I'm sorry; I seem to have forgotten my purse." She lowered her dispirited eyes, burning shame taking her for its own. She turned to go.

"Wait…wait, Emily. Here, have the bottle; I wouldn't want your party to go awry, for the sake of one measly bottle," to reassure her old neighbour and save her from any further embarrassment, she added, "Look, I'll put my own money into the till to cover; you can pay me back when you're passing the shop sometime and Mister Edwards, my boss, will be none the wiser."

"Th…thank you," stammered Emily grabbing the bottle, hiding it beneath her heavy coat and almost running out of the off-licence; the haunting echo of the tinkling bell like an ominous warning, merging together with the raw pain in her heart.

Each heavy step brought her closer to the house she yearned to run away from; the house she no longer thought as a secure, loving home. It was, she concluded, cracking at the seams and no amount of plastering would conceal the gaping holes that were growing ever wider. It was all falling apart; her relationship with Malcolm; her relationship with her son and the relationship, such as it had been, between Malcolm and Peter. Step by heavy step, her whirling thoughts accompanied each solitary step and, as her steps accumulated in number, so did her perturbed thoughts. Did Malcolm ever truly have a bond with Peter, or was it all an act; did he truly love her? Why did he want Peter out of the way; was it purely for academic purposes, or did he have a more sinister motive in mind? Who was the real Malcolm Mosterby? She asked herself over and over again and the more she asked, the more unsettling questions loomed on the horizon. Step by solitary step, her anxieties grew, until she came to an undeniable conclusion; she was losing her son and Malcolm, the man she loved, was the perpetrator of her loss.

Sliding her fingers into the opening of her coat, she touched the cool glass and immediately, as if touching a piece of burning coal, withdrew her trembling fingers. After seeing what the ravages of alcohol had done to her own father, she abhorred it with a passion, never touching the stuff.

Step by step, she walked down the familiar road of expensive detached residences; her eyes surveying, as if for the first time, their sheer exclusiveness and elegance only pots of money could buy. She let out a long sigh, ragged and deep. I don't belong here, she told herself. I never belonged here and I never will belong here. Suddenly the sense of being on the outside looking in enveloped her, suffusing all her senses with an urgency to run, she knew not where; anywhere; somewhere away from this road and all it represented. Her fingers re-entered the gap in her coat, digging into the deep inside pocket once more and she clasped the bottle tightly. She had heard the substance inside provided a sense of release and was already comforted by its promise. Placing one determined foot in front of the other, accelerating her speed, she wondered whether what people said about booze was actually true.

She saw him from afar and her heart froze. He was walking way in front of her in the same direction; both were heading for the same destination, a house she no longer considered her home.

Her eyes dropped to the jar dangling in his hand, swaying with each joyous step the youngster took and she wondered how many tadpoles Peter had caught, as her heart broke into a thousand bitter fragments.

The jar stood proudly on the large kitchen table; two pairs of inquisitive eyes staring unblinkingly at the small, black floating blobs inside; her ears attuned to the excited voices coming from the kitchen as she stood in its periphery, her stomach simultaneously churning and wrenching.

Slipping up the stairs unnoticed, she disposed of her *secret* into the laundry basket, knowing no one ever went near except to hastily dump in dirty clothes; ran down the stairs and stood at the door once more, peering at the two males and the jar of tadpoles, listening to Malcolm as he explained to Peter, in great detail, the life stages of a tadpole, while she glared at the scene and silently shouted, Don't listen to him, Peter; this is your betrayer. He's sending you away—away—away—

Feeling a presence excited eyes rose. "Mumm… Mummy, look what I've got!" He ran to her, his small hand grabbing hers and dragging her to the table, closer to the betrayer.

She sat, her eyes mesmerised by the small, black floating creatures, and like them, she felt caught, trapped, owned, enslaved waiting for fate to take its ultimate course; the loud ticking of the clock on the wall telling her that the *time* was drawing near. If only I was stronger. She shook her head, her eyes not leaving the blobs. If only I could stand up to him. If only—

But, there was a way to ease her pain. There was a way out.

Day by day, she felt him withdrawing from her, slowly and surely. When Peter was not at school, he was with Malcolm kicking a ball around the extensive, immaculately manicured, garden, or they were going fishing together or cleaning Malcolm's car together; Malcolm and his shadow. Malcolm and the boy he wanted out of the way, so he could have her all to himself, for he could never share a woman with anyone, no matter how old or young the contender.

On a rare occasion, two weeks before Peter's departure date, Emily espied her son on his own in the garden kicking a ball around. How young, innocent and vulnerable he looked, her thought propelling her to take steps towards him and, as he spotted her, he abandoned his football and ran to her side and hugged her tightly.

Seated on a rustic bench she took his small hands into her own, draining an inner comfort from their warmth. "Peter," she almost whispered.

Abruptly he turned to face her, his eyes wide. "Yes, Mummy?"

She gazed down at her son, her eyes lingering on the tufts of dark, unruly hair on his crown making her heart wrench and her guts twist. "Peter, do you really want to go to this new school?" Her eyes soaked his face.

"Yes, Mummy." He nodded his head vigorously and stopped as if a sudden thought had struck him; his innocent eyes rose to his mother. "Do you want me to go; will you be lonely without me, Mummy?"

This was her moment. Her mind raced. This was her moment to say, No…no, my precious one; I don't want you to leave me; I want you to be with me always and forever; I want us to run away from this pretentious neighbourhood and the haughty people who inhabit it; I want us to run away from all it stands for; away from Malcolm, far…far away.

"Mummy." She felt the tug of her cardigan sleeve, her watery eyes looking steadily at her son. "Don't you want me to go, Mummy?" She heard his soft voice as it lacerated her raw heart and heard the distant echo of her own words.

"I want you to be happy, Peter."

"I will be happy; I will be happy, Mummy. Malcolm says my new school has a big…huge swimming pool!"

She felt the warmth of his body leave her as he rose and ran back to his ball. She closed her eyes. Maybe, just maybe, she had got it all wrong; maybe she was seeing into things that were not there; maybe she had somehow got the whole thing out of perspective. Perhaps Malcolm wasn't the devil incarnate, after all; perhaps he was the good, caring man she had originally thought he was; perhaps he was only looking out for his charge's interests; perhaps he wanted the best for them all; perhaps she had been in the wrong; perhaps Malcolm was their saviour, after all. From that moment on, she began to see things in a different way; setting aside her own grief at Peter's impending departure and doing all in her power to make his paths straighter.

The day of departure arrived, and though the sun filtered through the curtains, a secret sorrow resided deep in the depth of Emily's heart for, she knew, that from this day forth things would never be the same again. How could they be the same? Peter was leaving her.

The drive down to Oxford, and the exclusive boys' boarding school, was full of chattering, laughter and lively background music. With each kilometre nearer to their destination, Emily's heart was torn more and more and she knew the gaping raw wound would never be healed, no matter how much her son enjoyed his new school; no matter how many examinations he passed with flying colours, or however many sporting trophies he acquired, for a part of him would leave her forever and no matter how many times, or how frequently he came home, it would never be to stay. Things would never be the same again.

She closed her eyes, a thousand distant memories flooding into the forefront of her mind, each vying for her exclusive attention. Ralph Brook's image was as clear as day. Ralph Brooke, Peter's biological father, was tall, well-built and handsome with his thick crop of dark hair and sparkling eyes. Ralph Brooke a kind, honest, caring, respectable and reliable man, until the day he walked out on his son. Ralph Brooke; Peter's father; what would he have to say about all this? Would he be bothered to say anything at all, after all, it was he who had walked away from them. Squeezing her eyes tightly to obliterate his image, she drew in a heavy ragged breath. Why did he walk out on them? She opened her eyes wide as the car came to a silent, decisive stop. "We're here, Peter," she heard the damning words; the words that would seal her son's future.

Her eyes scanned the ancient sprawling brownstone building and perfectly manicured grounds; the expensive motors rolling along the long, curved drive; the pretentious people, so full of only themselves, their wealth and status to see beyond their futile lives, stepping out their gleaming cars and depositing their offspring on to others, while they rushed back to their lavish dinner parties,

90

expensive trips abroad and exclusive golfing tournaments, where there was no room or time for their kids. And she to others, she dismally concluded, would be assessed in exactly the same way; for, how could they know that inside her heart was breaking into a thousand jagged shards, her spirit dying and her mind thinking only of the unopened bottle, deep in the secret depths of the laundry basket.

The long drive home was interrupted only by the sounds of the DJ and his music. Malcolm had made a couple of tentative attempts at conversing with his partner, failed miserably and left Emily to stew in her own thoughts.

She stared unblinkingly out the window at the passing shorn fields, the passing silver ribbons of lazy meandering rivers weaving this way and that, unsightly high-rise monstrosities and an assortment of cars, lorries, vans and coaches speeding by. She saw nothing but her precious, darling son standing rigidly outside the solid oak door, next to a complete stranger and waving his small hand. *Bye Mummy. Bye...bye...bye...* His last words still reverberated in her ears; she held on to them before burying the treasured words deep in her pained heart. Goodbye, Peter, she had whispered.

Erratically, she had tossed and turned throughout the long, torturous night, thoughts of Peter her only constant companion. He would be asleep now, her wandering thoughts decided. Will he be tucked up in a single bed in a dormitory or sharing a bunk bed; will he be safe and warm; will he be hungry; did he have a glass of milk before he went to bed; does he have a new friend; is he thinking of me? Who; what; why; where; when; how? Questions followed questions until they all merged together in her exhausted head.

Glancing sideways at a sleeping Malcolm, she lightly moved her cover to one side, crept out of the room and opened the door of Peter's bedroom, his private sanctuary. Step by slow step, she ventured inside; stealthily as if he was asleep in his bed; as if she did not want to arouse him from his slumber. Perching on the end of his bed, she clicked on his bed-table lamp, the light subdued beneath the Batman shade. His superhero was everything to him. She smiled, as she wondered whether he'd been allowed to cover his bed with his Batman and Robin bedspread. Closing her eyes she imagined him in his room.

Smoothing her hand over his cool pillow she speculated, which pair of pyjamas he had decided to wear on his first night away from home, as her eyes scanned the library of books, most of them about superheroes, though there were a few on the solar system and she spotted one on frogs, making her smile instantly disappear, as Malcolm's words pierced her thoughts… We have found a fantastic school for you, Peter; a school you will do very well in; a school you will be very happy at… His echoing words seared through her heart, more lethal than the blade could ever be and with them came the surge of agonising pain; raw, undiluted pain bringing into focus the bottle deep in the depths of its secret hiding place, making her heart pump erratically, obliterating all other thoughts until the bottle seemed to cry out to her; creating in her an excruciating burning need that she knew could only be extinguished by consuming the liquid inside. No. She clenched her eyes tightly shaking her head. She would not go there; it was not the answer, besides she hated the disgusting stuff. Focusing her eyes directly on her son's study table, she willed with all her might for the burning urge to go away, her feet following her eyes.

On his neatly arranged desk was a small pile of neatly stacked textbooks, his globe, a pencil and pen holder and, resting behind the globe, a closed notebook. Her eyes lingered on the cover, depicting an image of a man in a cape and mask. She took the notebook and flicked the cover open, her eyes instantly widening. "A journal!" She exclaimed, her fingers rapidly withdrawing, her feet taking steps back, her body lowering again onto Peter's bed, as she purposefully withdrew herself from his little private world, though her eyes continued to stare at the opened notebook. "A journal," she whispered. She hadn't had an inkling.

Snatching the notebook, she hastily placed it back down again behind the globe and closed the door on Peter's world; the world he did not wish to share with anyone but his superhero.

In the silence and solitude of the large house, serenity evaded Emily as tormented, chaotic thoughts wrestled with her emotions, making them flit erratically and uncontrollably in her head. One minute she was happy in having the whole house to herself, happy in the knowledge that her son was having the best all-round education money could afford and happy that Malcolm spent long days and evenings at the office; the next minute she felt utterly abandoned, alone and lonely; unwanted and not needed; a waste of space.

It was as she was feeling at her lowest, her fingers clutching tightly around an untouched mug of black coffee, her visionless eyes staring into stark oblivion, that the thought stealthily sneaked its way into her head and Peter's journal loomed clear in her mind and, with it, came her boy's smiling image; young eyes twinkling, two delightful dimples in his cheeks, as he smiled at her and the question crushed into her thoughts. Why did he feel the need to keep a journal? *Many children keep a journal*, a logical voice in her head replied. Why didn't he want me to know about it? *Because he wanted to keep it a secret*, the voice echoed…*secret…secret…secret…*

The resounding echo boomed loudly and clearly. "A secret," she reiterated, her eyes looking down at Batman looking up at her. He didn't want to tell me certain things. Her heart twisted. He felt he couldn't share secrets…*secrets…secrets…secrets…*the voice echoed faithfully until she felt her whole head exploding and, with it, her broken heart.

Fingers opened the cover, her impulsive eyes lowered onto the page of untidy scrawl and she began to read silently… *Deer Batman,* she smiled and continued, *Mummy is bayking my favurat buns—choclat buns with lots and lots and lots of choclat sprinkls. Ill sayv yoo and Robin som. Bye for naw. Your frend, Peter x…* He always was such a generous little boy, but an atrocious speller, she smiled and flicked the page… *Deer Batman and Robin, My mummy bowt my favurat comic today—the one yor in. Cant wayt to reed al abowt you. I luv Mummy. I luv yoo and Robin. Peter x…* She felt the tug in her heart.

"I love you too, Son," she said aloud before her fingers flicked to the next page… *Deer Batman, I am having sosages and mash for tee. Do yoo like lyk sosages? Ill sayv yoo and Robin som. Yor frend. Peter…* She flicked a few more pages before her eyes espied a page depicting an array of red love hearts around some text, making her brow furrow. Could her young, innocent boy have fallen in love? She smiled shaking her head and continued to read the sprawling, untidy handwriting… *Batman, I hav very important neews to tell yoo and I wont to no wat you think. Mummy has got a boyfrend. His got a nys smyl. Mummy is smyling a lot too. Peter x…* The smile around Emily's mouth faded and disappeared, but still, her fingers turned the pages and stopped…

Deer Batman and Robin, Mummys boyfrend is gowing to be my gardyan. I wish yoo cood com to my mummys weding. I cant wayt. Peter x PS Ill sayv yoo som weding cayk… It was, she reflected, an innocent Peter who had alerted her attention to Malcolm; it was Peter who had warmed to him first and it was with Peter's consent that she had moved in with this man. She would do all for Peter. And yet…and yet—Peter was the one who was now ensconced far away in a boys' boarding school. She felt a heavy cloak of sadness envelop her; thick and overwhelming shrouding her mind and soul and creating in her heart a hollow which nobody but Peter could fill.

Her mind drifted to Malcolm. Not a friend, neither a trusted confidante, merely a man she and her son lived with; a man she saw less and less, as he *worked* later and later into the evenings and night and, when she dared to tackle him about his late hours, he turned his icy eyes on her and snapped, "Somebody has to pay for the boy's education," before turning her back on her and switching off the bedside light.

The book slid from her lap alerting her to the present. Picking up the journal, and its secrets, she placed it under the globe and switched off the light.

One—two—three—four—five—The snores were ragged, loud and irregular making her turn her eyes on him and glare at the stubble on his face peeping through; his eyes closed to the world; his body shut to her needs and wants. She closed her eyes trying to remember the exact time he changed towards her. First, there was the irregular sex until that dwindled into none at all; next came the late evenings at work and, the night before last, he failed to come home at all; the scent of faint expensive perfume on his jacket, his shirt. She did not interrogate him; there was, she thought, no point. He would only come up with some viable *reason*, making her feel as if she was intruding into his business. And so she kept her silence, her own senses telling her everything she needed to know for her eyes had seen the red lipstick on his shirt collar, her nose had smelt the perfume and her ears had heard the casual snippets of gossip.

For the second time, she threw the duvet to one side and stepped into the shower cubicle, turned on the knob to full power and stood under the powerful thrust of the cascading water, allowing it to wash over her hair, face, arms legs; willing the water to wash away all her worries, fears, anxieties and insecurities; to wash away her guilt and make her clean on the inside as well as the outside. Closing her eyes, she revelled in the sound of the rushing water; the feel of the splintered sheets of liquid as it fell—fell—fell on top and around her; closing her into a liquified cocoon, where she gradually began to feel free of strife; free of guilt; free.

His cough alerted her to the fact that he was awake. Quickly, she smothered her shapely body with gel and allowed the jet stream to rinse away the orange-scented substance, vigorously she rubbed herself down and proceeded to dress.

"Good morning," he mumbled avoiding her eyes.

"What time will you be home tonight, Malcolm?" She asked cautiously, staring unblinkingly at his back.

"Whatever time will be the time, Emily," he snapped, his cold response indicating there was no more to say on the subject; it was closed.

In the depths of her cold, lonely heart there was a gram of comfort. She would not be alone, not now that she had a secret part of Peter that nobody could take away from her; nobody.

The *click* of the outside door, the sound of retreating footsteps on the gravel, filled her heart with relief and, as the ignition started in Malcolm's expensive motor, Emily's feet ran up the stairs and into her son's bedroom. Withdrawing Peter's secret book, she sat comfortably in his easy chair and opened the cover, rapidly flicking through the pages to the place she had stopped reading, her eyes glued to the page as she absorbed his words… *Batman… Robin. I hav som important neews to tel yoo…* Her eyes moved eagerly on, her heart rapidly freezing as her lips read… *I hav a reely big broblem. Malcom is sending me of to skool far away and I dont wont to go. I dont wont to leev Mummy and I don't wont to go. Yoov got sooper powers Batman. Pleez help me. Peter x…*

Her freezing heart shattered into a thousand jagged splinters, her guts numb. Raising her eyes she reread the extract, hoping to read a different set of words, but her eyes remained solidly fixed on the undeniable words and the undeniable truth behind them… *I don't wont to leev Mummy and I don't wont to go… I don't wont to leev… I don't wont to go… I don't wont to leev…* His young, innocent confession penetrated and echoed loudly in her head, took root and reverberated in her broken heart; the words wrapping tightly and mercilessly around her twisting guts, invading her guilt-ridden eyes and re-entering her iced heart, where they remained.

The journal landed with a thud on the carpet, as her feet rushed out of his room and into her own room and stopped abruptly. Slowly lifting the lid, her trembling fingers dug deep—deeper until they clashed with the cool glass. Carefully she lifted the bottle out, her heart pounding furiously as she walked back into her son's room and placed the bottle on his night table, next to Peter's treasured globe.

Sitting on the bed she stared unflinchingly at the unopened bottle; it was clear, still liquid untouched as she wondered what on earth people found so fascinating, so alluring about alcohol. Her eyes lowered to the upturned book on the floor, Batman staring up at her, Peter's words seeping into her mind… *Yoov got sooper powers, Batman. Pleez help me…* She shook her head slowly from side to side. If only—Her eyes drifted back to the bottle and lowered back to the book. Picking the journal up, she rested it on her lap, her tightly clenched hands resting on the cover, her mind whirling erratically with mixed questions and subconscious statements. Should she read on? These were Peter's secrets; secrets he wanted to share with no one, but his superhero. Should she read on? What if there was something more in there that she needed to know; what if there wasn't?

Flicking to an unread page, her eyes rested on the first word of the first line and laboriously she read on… '*Deer Batman. Mummy hates me and she is sending me away. My skool work is rubish and I am no good and I hav to go away. I am gowing to tayk yoo with me. Yor frend Peter x…*' "He forgot to take you, Batman," she stated aloud. The blade plunged deep and hard; it ripped, shred and tore without mercy creating a numbness and rawness within her that she knew could never be remedied.

Frantically, as if she was running out of time, she impatiently unscrewed the metal top. "Damn," she cursed. "The glass." But the overwhelming need inside her heart, guts, head and soul overpowered the etiquette to drink from an appropriate receptacle. Bringing the bottle up to her mouth, she took one large gulp, swallowed it, coughed and spluttered as she felt its burning rawness, and allowed the remnants to slither down her throat, instantly creating a feeling of unfamiliar, welcome warmth and with that warmth came comfort which dispelled the edge of raw pain. Taking another generous swallow, she lowered herself into Peter's easy chair, closed her eyes and let the liquid do its magic.

The faint chiming of the clock downstairs propelled her eyelids to open, her reluctant body to rise and her mind to change course. She had a house to tidy and a garden to maintain; she had long ago dispersed the housekeeper and gardener, insisting that while she had her health and time, there was no need for others to do her work. Good, solid work, whatever form it took, dispelled the demons away, she always maintained, and today was going to be no different. The uncharacteristic weakness she had succumbed to, she firmly concluded, was just that; an uncharacteristic, temporary weakness; something, she vowed, she would never succumb to again. She was strong.

Her diligent fingers went back and forth, tugging and pulling, throwing the weeds into a nearby refuse container, which was already full of discarded weeds and dead branches; her mind solely on the job in hand, denying it the indulgence of wandering into forbidden territory. Swiftly plucking a handful of dandelions out of their resting place and slinging them on top of the heap, her eyes spotted something in the hedgerow; her eyes narrowing, a frown etching on her forehead, she rose and approached the mysterious object, her body stooping, her eyes scrutinising, her heart stopping as her fingers withdrew the item and a smile broke out on her lips as memories, of her son and Malcolm kicking Peter's ball about, flooded into her mind; happy, sunny days when Peter had not been forced to go to a place where he did not want to go. The familiar knife plunged and twisted until she felt she could not breathe, for the brutal twist was suffocating her. Dropping the ball and her gardening gloves onto the grass, she turned and ran up to the house, up the stairs and into her bedroom. "Malcolm!" She exclaimed her eyes as wide as saucers.

"I forgot some papers." He held his reclaimed evidence mid-air. "I'll see you later."

"What time will you…" The *click* of the outside door interrupted her flow of words, just as Malcolm had interrupted her dash for alcohol. Her eyes flitted to the laundry basket. The ravenous, gnawing need slowly ebbed away. The laundry basket remained closed.

Days passed. Letters from Peter drifted through the letter box; happy, childish letters full of news about his new-found friends, his football team and the large swimming pool in the school. Peter, she concluded, was happy and that was all that mattered. All that he had written in his journal; all his worries were now in the past. Peter was happy.

The journal remained closed and the liquor remained hidden in the depths of its secret hiding place and Emily resigned herself to a solitary, empty and lonely life; totally oblivious to the fact that, hundreds of kilometres away, her son had buried his head under his pillow and was sobbing his heart out, his whole world crumbling around him as he yearned to be back home with his mum and in the sanctuary of his bedroom with all his treasures around him.

Peter Brooke was picked on, bullied and ostracised by the boys who thought he was beneath them. They laughed and poked fun at him for saving and protecting an injured bird; they jeered at him for his excitement over a Brimstone butterfly and scoffed at him rescuing a spider, from having his legs torn off for fun. He was not *one of them.* He did not conform. He was lower-class, a bore, and an outsider. He did not belong.

Like a burst of sunshine after a storm, his superhero crashed into his bleak thoughts and a rare smile broke forth, his hand roughly swiping the salty tears from his pale cheeks. Abruptly he rose from his bed, retrieved a writing pad and pen and started to write to his special, secret friend… *Deer Batman. I am lonly heer. I hayt it heer. I hate everybody heer. I wont to go hom. Yoo are my only frend. Peter x*... Immediately, a heavy weight lifted and another smile dared to dance on his lips, as he placed the letter under his pillow.

Malcolm stayed longer and later at *work* and the nights he didn't come home at all rapidly increased in number and frequency until it became the norm.

Emily spent her evenings writing long letters to Peter; reading novel after novel from cover to cover, regardless of the story being good, bad or indifferent; watching the television and waiting—waiting for the door to open and Malcolm to magically reappear.

The door remained firmly shut; the phone rested still and silent in its cradle; the silence around her was deafening, as she screamed inwardly for some kind of release from her lonely prison and then—and then—she remembered.

Padding across the room the heavy, excruciating blanket of unbearable emptiness was already beginning to lift, releasing a smile on her lips as her fingers lifted the wicker lid and delved deep—deep—until they touched, clutched and withdrew the cool, smooth glass bottle.

For long seconds, her unflinching eyes stared at the bottle of clear liquid, her breathing heavy and laborious; her senses fighting a ravenous war with her inner self. Closing her eyelids, her mouth set into a firm, thin line; her tense body heaved a heavy, jagged sigh, as her mind played a series of contradictory scenarios and pursued the one where she was unscrewing the metal top and tipping the potent liquid into her waiting mouth. One overriding thought remained clear; peace; peace in her tortured soul, heart and soul; peace. Guilt, she knew, would rear its ugly head and kill her peace but, for now, the temptation to succumb was greater. Cool, silky, inviting her temptress was offering her the world; promising to banish her anxieties, fears and insecurities; vowing to be her best friend. *No one would ever know...no one would ever know...no one would ever know...*her alluring words echoed in Emily's head, becoming louder and louder, clearer and more convincing with each echo. "No one would ever know," she stated loudly, her hand bringing the bottle up to her opened mouth. The vodka slithered down her throat like smooth liquid-silk, immediately creating a comforting blanket of soothing warmth around her and a new resolve, to cope with anything life had to throw at her.

Eagerly, she read Peter's short letters. He was happy; she smiled, knowing that his all-too-brief notes were due to the fact that his days were so full; he had no time to scribe lengthy and detailed accounts.

Malcolm made brief appearances, specifically for a quick shower, to change his clothes and to pick up certain items he needed. Just as quickly he disappeared. The lingering scent on his shirt propelled Emily to transfer her allegiance from her husband and onto the bottle, which quickly became her loyal friend; the only friend she had.

Emily's red-blotched eyes stared at the gilt-edged invitation as simultaneously her heart soared and deflated. Pouring herself a generous measure of clear liquid, she sat at the kitchen table, took a mouthful and studied the card, feeling the potency of the alcohol creating its magic, allowing her heart to dance. A smile rose to her lips. She would be seeing Peter again. Clasping the card tightly to her chest she closed her eyes and whispered, "Peter, my precious, precious son." Taking another substantial swig, she stowed the bottle away, propped the invitation on the marble mantelpiece and got on with the daily chores, with an added amount of zest and Peter's image dancing in her head.

His cold, detached eyes took in the words; her excited sighs and words made his guts twist and cringe. The last thing on earth he wanted was to drive down to Oxford and play happy families with a so-called partner he did not love and a brat he did not care one iota about for, as far as he was concerned, the moment he had deposited the sprog at the door of the exclusive boarding school, was the moment he had transferred his responsibilities on to others. Out of sight, out of mind, was his motto. Besides, he incorrigibly concluded that he now had another new family, Angela and her two children, and the sooner he could get rid of Emily and her sprog, the better.

The ninth of December was ingrained in Emily's heart, soul, brain and being. Five weeks and three days to go; she wondered how many hours, minutes, seconds. Slipping into her cold, lonely bed she resolved to throw away her bottle, with its remaining contents, first thing in the morning.

Thirty-eight days; Peter had meticulously penned the strokes on his calendar. Thirty-eight days before he saw his mum; thirty-eight days before he could hug her and kiss her and tell her how much he hated this place and beg her to take him home with her and Malcolm; thirty-eight days—only thirty-eight days and tomorrow it would be thirty-seven days. It wasn't long, he shook his head from side to side; but, it still felt like an eternity.

Humming happily to herself, Emily deftly separated the laundry lights from the darks, her fingers rummaging in pockets for any forgotten bits of anything, before she bunged the garments into the washing machine. Her swift searching fingers stopped and withdrew, her inquisitive eyes scrutinising carefully the small card in her hand; *The Sands Hotel;* another pocket, another card; *Peacock Hotel, Brighton.* A pair of black trousers and a lipstick-smeared handkerchief stuffed into the depths of the pocket, followed by a shirt, bearing the faintest remnants of scent. She rose and stood perfectly still with the shirt tightly clasped in her trembling fingers, her eyes closed against the undeniable evidence all around her; a tsunami of truths uncovered and the stark certainty that Malcolm did not love her anymore.

The laundry lid was discarded on the floor; fingers dug deep, the liquid slid down her gullet; another mouthful followed and another and another, forcing Malcolm's deceitful image into insignificance as a mellow, warm feeling spread over her, wrapping its tentacles around her; taking her for its own.

Everything was right with the world, as she lay on the bed she had shared with Malcolm and allowed the fuzziness to overtake her.

"What the fucking hell is this?"

Laboriously her exhausted eyes opened, confronted by a dark figure looming over her with an empty bottle waving in his hand. Eyes flickered; a heart pounded. "I...er... I..."

"You're fucking drunk!" Roared Malcolm; his threatening, exasperated eyes fixed on the woman below him.

"I... I..." She attempted to heave herself up onto one elbow, fatigue taking over and forcing her to lie back down.

"You're fucking drunk, woman, in the middle of the frigging day!"

Her hand clutching tightly onto the banister, one wobbly foot placed cautiously in front of the other, she meekly followed him down the stairs, her eyes witnessing the exact scene which had greeted her husband's astounded eyes some minutes earlier; clothes strewn unwashed and discarded on the floor and there, before her very eyes, a lipstick-smeared shirt.

"You're a fucking disgrace, Emily." He sneered, his disdainful eyes looking her up and down.

"And you're playing away," she said in a soft, almost inaudible voice.

He turned on her, his eyes ablaze. "Do you blame me; do you fucking well blame me when I have a lush for a partner?" He continued to stare at her, his eyes boring into her very soul; the so-called love he once had for her was well and truly gone. Turning he picked up his holdall and walked towards the door. Turning he snapped, "And, if you think I am taking a drunkard down to Oxford with me, you can think again."

The bang of the door reverberated in her ears ten-fold, her eyes lowering to an assortment of proof, regarding Malcolm's infidelity, staring up at her and the feel of a sharp, serrated blade thrusting deep—deep—deep into the depths of her pained heart, which only one type of medicine could heal.

Her heart pounding, she staggered back up the stairs, withdrew a secreted half-filled bottle from the bowels of her wardrobe and drank in greedy mouthfuls, closing her eyes tightly and willing the numbness to, once again, overtake her senses.

It evaded her. Instead, the potency of the alcohol brought with it a deeper clarification of the raw pain slashing her troubled heart… *And if you think I am taking a drunkard down to Oxford with me, you can think again*… His damning words hammered in her head. He didn't mean it, she told herself. He's said things before in the heat of the moment and didn't mean them. He didn't mean it—He didn't mean it—He did not mean it! *He did mean it*, a voice contradicted sharply, *He did mean it!*

Her hungry eyes drifted to the empty abandoned bottle on her bed, an uncontrollable urge for the need of another drink rising; a persuasive voice in her head telling her *it* would make things better; she would be able to see things from a clearer perspective. "I need a drink." She heard the echo of her own words. "I need a damn drink—now!"

Smiling victoriously, her feet headed for the cabinet, and grabbing a bottle of Malcolm's finest malt whisky, she headed for Peter's room. Picking up his journal she sat in his rocking chair, opened the cover and read… '*Deer Batman. Thank yoo for being my frend. Withowt yoo I woodnt hav a frend. Mummy is too bizy with Malcom and Malcom wonts to send me away. They don't wont me to liv heer anymore. Yor frend. Peter x…*' The familiar sharp blade thrust deep once more, her fingers curled tightly around the opened bottle as she brought it up to her waiting mouth… *And if you think I'm taking a drunkard… Mummy is too bizy with Malcom… Malcom wonts to send me away… Your fucking drunk…*

They don't wont me heer… And if you think… The oral and written words merged together going round and round in her head until finally, sweet oblivion took her, once more, for its own.

He stared out the leaded window as gleaming, expensive cars glided into the drive and designer-attired parents alighted and greeted their waiting sons. His expectant eyes strained further into the distance, then lowered to his watch. The performance would be starting in twenty minutes. He should be backstage. There were no more cars appearing but his young, hopeful heart refused to give up and his eyes eventually saw what he was looking for in the far, far distance as the motor approached a distant curve of the long, sweeping drive. "They're here! They're here!" He shouted excitedly as he jumped frantically from foot to foot, his eyes alive and sparkling. "Mummy and Malcolm are here! I knew they'd come… I just knew they'd come."

Words crashed into untold joy. "Peter, it is time to go, they need you."

He felt urgent eyes on him, but his eyes remained firmly fixed on the slow-approaching vehicle, admonishing himself severely for ever doubting them.

Young eyes followed Malcolm, his impatient feet itching to run to the gleaming motor and hug tightly his mother; a sheen of puzzlement veiling his eyes as his guardian walked purposefully towards him, alone. His young heart plummeted to the depths of an empty, cold, lonely place; an all too familiar place. He opened his mouth and closed it, his heart clenching tightly as he heard the words. "I am sorry, Peter, your mother couldn't come."

Cold, stark words uttered in a cold, stark manner coming from the mouth of a stark, cold man.

"Why couldn't Mummy come, Malcolm?"

The young boy's words were met with a wall of silence as feet stepped into the grand building and ears were immediately bombarded with happy, excited voices.

After the successful performance, as parents and pupils partook in a lavish spread, Malcolm took Peter into a small side room, pre-arranged by the head teacher at Malcolm's request.

Wide eyes stared at the older man, lowering to his large, broad hands clasped together on the polished table, Peter's logical mind telling him that Mummy couldn't come to the concert because she was busy at home preparing for his homecoming after reading his letter, in which he told her how very unhappy he was at the school.

The following three weeks saw three lives change dramatically and irrevocably forever.

Green, wide eyes stared at the middle-aged woman's tightly permed hair and he wondered how she managed to get it so very curly when Mummy's hair was always so straight and kind of silky. Looking at the woman's thin, determined face, he also wondered what he was doing walking away from his posh school with this complete stranger; but, he had seen her talking to his head teacher so, he guessed, she was ok. Perhaps, she was going to take him home, back to Mummy. Climbing into the back seat of her small car, his eyes watched her long fingers unfold a piece of paper and study it, before turning on the ignition and driving away.

It was a long journey past fields, through traffic-congested towns and bypassing cities and the longer they travelled, the bigger Peter's smile became. I am going home to my mummy, he concluded, as a flurry of joyful butterflies danced in his tummy, his young heart beating with wild anticipation. At a set of traffic lights, the woman darted a cursory glance at her young passenger, her thin lips remaining firmly clamped, the blanket of air around them heavy as the car purred onwards.

Peter's young mind drifted to a happy home and happy, sunny times when Malcolm and he played football or snakes and ladders; when Mummy hummed whilst washing the pots; when they all went to the beach, caught crabs in buckets and paddled in the sea; when Malcolm helped him to make the biggest and grandest sandcastle; when they all ate fish and chips and lots of fluffy pink candyfloss, happily reflecting on their day at the seaside. Soon, he'd be enjoying all these wonderful things again; a smile danced on his lips, his mind speculating what new adventures they could all experience together, as the car drove nearer and nearer to its destination; nearer and nearer towards home.

Decreasing speed the car came to a stop. Peter's eyes widened his brow furrowing, his whole body turning this way and that to get a better view; a different view. "Where are we, Miss?"

"Home," she answered curtly.

Home, his brow furrowed once more. It must be her home, he thought, and before his mind wandered further, she opened the car door and ushered him out.

The firm knocks on the door brought out another thin woman. A lady who did not look at all friendly, he judged looking up at her stern face, her thin lips and her eyes which looked positively evil.

"This is your new home, Peter," stated his chauffeur, and before he could ask her any questions, she was briskly walking down the short drive and he, and his battered suitcase, were left on the doorstep, with the unfriendly-looking stranger-looking down on him.

"You better come in," she said briskly.

Peter's face visibly paled before her close-knit eyes. "This is not my house, lady," he stated defiantly, looking up at her shrewd eyes.

"It is now, get in." She roughly grabbed hold of his arm and hauled him inside into the grimy, dimly lit hallway.

"I want to go home—I want to go home." He wriggled this way and that, trying to escape the clutches of her tight grip on him.

"Get the fuck in!" She snarled, pushing him further into the house and into a grubby room, where he came face-to-face with a chubby, stern-faced man in his mid to late forties, sitting in an upright chair.

"What the hell do we have here, Rose?" He sneered, his tobacco-stained teeth showing.

She heaved heavily as if to catch her breath, releasing her grip on Peter. "One of our Malcolm's cast-offs," she stated abruptly, staring venomously at the young lad as one would look down on a despicable worm.

Icy shivers ran up and down Peter's body, as he stood trembling beneath her inhospitable gaze, his young heart racing, his watery eyes switching to the uncouth man in a stained, stripy shirt and a day's stubble on his chubby chin. Eyes stared at eyes; young and old; old and young; both wishing the other would disappear. Words escaped before Peter could clamp them down. "I want to go home, mister," he stated, his upper lip trembling as he desperately tried to restrain the glistening tears from falling. They fell and his voice trembled in unison with his upper lip. "I want to go home to…to my mummy."

"Rose, get him out of my fucking sight, now!" bellowed the man, slamming his tightly clenched fist on the table, sending a cup rattling against a saucer.

The tightly clenched fingers around his thin arms, made a fresh load of shivers invade Peter's body; making his guts writhe and twist before bundling together into a tight knot, which seemed to rise from the bowels of his stomach to his pounded throat, suffocating him. "I want t…to go home." He managed to squeeze the stuttering words out. The hard slap on his face made his heart stop momentarily and his young mind whirl in a hazy blur until he was conscious of nothing and no one.

Sometime later, his eyes slowly opened and flickered to a high, stained ceiling and garish wallpaper which was also stained, depicting large grotesque flowers he could not identify. His eyes stared at one such unsightly image; yellow, spiky and ugly.

"Hello."

The soft voice went through him like a tornado, thrusting him sharply into the here and now. "Where am I?" He dared to ask, his voice faint and almost inaudible; his eyes searching in the dimness for the owner of the voice.

"You're in Uncle Damian and Auntie Rose's house," replied the softly-spoken voice; a girl's voice.

... Uncle Damian and Auntie Rose... Uncle Damian and Auntie Rose... He sat up bolt upright, his eyes finally locating a bundle on a bed on the opposite side of the room, while his buzzing head searched desperately for a meaning; any association he may have had with Uncle Damian and Auntie Rose, his head slowly shaking from side to side. "I haven't got an Auntie Rose and Uncle Damian," he said, knowing he would have remembered them if his mother had ever mentioned them to him—unless—unless, maybe Malcolm—Squeezing his eyes tight he urged his fuzzy brain to remember.

There were questions to be asked; lots and lots and lots of questions. His discerning eyes opened and remained fixed on the partly covered bundle, noticing a crop of blonde hair sticking out from beneath the cover. "Why am I here?"

"Dunno."

"When am I going home?"

"Dunno."

"Do you live here?"

"Yep."

"Where are your mummy and daddy?"

The door opened. Peter's eyes darted to a figure hunched at a table and was engrossed in homework, "Lights out at nine o'clock sharp."

"I want to go home," Peter reiterated.

"Stop whining, boy." The door banged hard behind her, leaving the young boy to stare disdainfully at the thin slices of bread, spread with a slither of red substance which, Peter assumed, to be some sort of inferior jam. His face contorted into lines of grimacing disapproval, his mind thinking the snack looked absolutely disgusting, his eyes switching back to the bundle rapidly rising and hastily rushing over to the tray of meagre, unappetising offerings; his astonished eyes widening at the sight of a young girl of about twelve or thirteen, with straggly blonde hair, a very thin drawn face and the biggest, bluest eyes he had ever seen.

"You better have some," she stated, greedily grabbing two pieces of bread. "The tray will be taken away in five minutes time and then you won't have a thing until tomorrow morning."

His stomach gnawed and rumbled with hunger like he'd never known before, as his eyes stared contemptuously at the cracked plate with its unappetising fare. His body flopped down on the bed and he turned his head to the wall.

"Please yourself." The young girl nonchalantly shrugged her scrawny shoulders. "I'll have yours if you don't want it." Her thin fingers were already reaching out for Peter's portion.

He heard the *click* of the door, footsteps approaching, stopping, retreating; the switch of the light and he closed his eyes to the darkness shrouding him. I am in prison, he sobbed bitterly into his stained pillow. A sudden thought struck him. What would Batman do? Laying rigidly in the dark, he thought and thought and then, the answer came.

With the answer came a set of queries. How was he to escape; where would he go; how far was home; how would he get there; what would he tell Mummy and—Malcolm? These questions and more he put on the back burner of his mind. Now, he told himself, he needed to sleep and tomorrow he would eat. He would need the energy to make his escape successful.

Sleep was an elusive stranger. Eyes wide open and prickly, he stared into an array of conflicting, distorted images weaving and interweaving; locking and interlocking; joining together and drifting independently apart, but all starred two main characters; Emily and Malcolm; together and apart; smiling and stern-faced, whirling and twisting; their images becoming grotesque and blurry, like the characters out of a horror movie, until he could recognise them no more; so horribly deformed they had become. He closed his weary eyes. Why weren't they here; why weren't they rescuing him, taking him home, feeding him with shepherd's pie and strawberry trifle, playing snakes and ladders, football, rugby, tucking him up in bed, planning exciting trips to the seaside together? Where were they; why had they abandoned him in this despicable dump? His heavy head buzzing he sprang out of bed, his hand on the doorknob.

"And where do you think you are going?"

Frozen, his iced body stood to immediate attention, as if he had been caught in some sort of unsavoury act by a fearsome sergeant major; his feet suddenly turned into two blobs of jelly, as he felt his insides writhe and twist and his heart cry silently, I want to go home; I want to be with my mummy.

"Where were you thinking of going?" The cold, harsh voice repeated.

"I… I was going to the toilet," Peter lied, bitterly dejected that his secret escape had been thwarted.

"It's here." The girl thrust into his trembling hand what seemed to be a bucket. "Piss in there and get back into bed, if you know what's good for you."

He climbed back into bed without pissing and clamped his eyes shut silently asking, *where are you, Batman, when I need you?*

The morning brought with it sunshine, hope and a stern warning from the young girl. Raising her eyes from her thinly buttered round of burnt toast, she fixed her eyes firmly on Peter. "Eat as much as you can at school." Turning, her ravenous mouth chewed greedily her meagre ration.

Wide-eyed he stared at her. "School?" He hadn't figured out how to go to school. He had thought only of going home; going home to his beloved mum, his room, football and his friend, Billy.

He was the only boy in the entire school who was not wearing at least part of the school uniform and he stuck out like a sore thumb; a spectacle who was immediately targeted, picked on, cajoled, teased and bullied. At the end of any given day, he was physically and mentally, visibly and invisibly, tormented; the mental scars leaving a mark on him for many years to come.

"You've got to stand up for yourself and fight back," Sally, his roommate told him. "If you don't you're going to sink, mate."

He sank. His body, heart and soul sank into the deep depths of despair; deeper and deeper until he felt he could swim against the tide no more and so, he turned against the tide; turned away from the world and started to withdraw into himself, into his shell where he knew he would be safe, secure and where no one could get to him. But before he reached his safe haven, he had one stubborn obstacle to manoeuvre and this stubborn obstacle was not going to give up without a fight.

Since her guardian had abandoned her and left her to rot at Uncle Damian and Auntie Rose's house, Sally had no one. Now, she had Peter and she was not going to let him go. He was, she determined, going to stay with her, whether he wanted to or not. There was no way she was going to allow him to simply withdraw and leave her alone and lonely and, being a very intelligent youngster, she knew that to get him on her side she would have to win his trust so she immediately set to work. "My guardian didn't want me either," she stated starkly, her observant eyes fixed on her self-appointed charge, making him throw invisible daggers her way.

"My guardian does want me and my mummy wants me," he yelled at the top of his voice, his pained eyes narrowing to mere slits.

"So where are they, Peter?"

His icy eyes stared at her and through her; wishing she was dead, while her haunting words echoed painfully in his ears…*where are they…where are they …where are they?…*

"They've abandoned you just like my guardian, Malcolm, abandoned me," she stated loudly, clearly lest he should mishear, or misinterpret her words.

"M… Malcolm," he stammered, "my guardian is called Malcolm too." His voice was quiet, almost inaudible.

"Coincidence; a mere coincidence," she stated before picking up her chewed pen and continuing with her homework; her means of escape.

He stared at the hunched figure as she picked up a protractor and started to measure an angle. But, he thought, what if—what if her Malcolm and his Malcolm were the same man; after all, was it just a coincidence they had both ended up in the same house? What if—what if—what if?—His young head whirled and buzzed with a multitude of *what-ifs*, as he stared unblinkingly at the young mathematician at the scuffed table, who was totally oblivious to his secret dilemma.

Unbeknown to the youngsters, Auntie Rose and Uncle Damian were reluctant providers of the basic necessities of life; they were merely a stopgap, and as far as they were concerned, the sooner the burdensome kids were moved on, the better; they were in it purely for the dosh. Neither liked children nor wanted them in their home; they had been thrust upon them by one of Malcolm's associates and, as Auntie Rose owed her brother a massive favour, she found herself in no position to deny his request.

After long minutes, Peter tentatively asked, "What was your guardian like, Sally?"

His innocent words hit her like a devastating thunderbolt. Ignoring him, she turned her protractor this way and that; her intelligent, intent eyes focused on the task of forming an isosceles triangle with a protractor on a page; his words bringing dark memories, as she hastily scribbled a series of calculations, while the ominous silence surrounded them with its coarse, prickly blanket.

"What was your Malcolm like, Sally?" He dared to pursue his quest for an answer; his words louder and clearer, lest she had failed to hear him the first time.

She heard; the memory of the man he was referring to sending sharp, painful splinters of pain through her young heart; willing it to resume its numb status because then, at least, she would not feel; she would not hurt; she would not be forced to remember the man she so desperately wanted to forget; the man who had ruined her life and had ended her mother's life.

"Sal?" Peter's innocent eyes wavered on the girl.

She rose, throwing vile eyes at the young boy. "For God's sake, leave me alone, you little squirt. My guardian is none of your concern."

"He could be my guardian too." The quiet, almost inaudible, words escaped his mouth before he could stop them; before he had time to think; before he had a chance to calculate their effect on his new friend. He felt the sudden pain at the side of his head, as a thick textbook thudded onto the floor. Holding the side of his head with his hand, his hard, accusing eyes shot to Sally, as he yelled at the top of his voice. "What did you do that for, you nutter?" His eyes darted to the opening door.

"Shut the fucking hell up!" yelled a more threatening voice, propelling young eyes to rise to Damian, before Peter's ears heard the damning words. "And, if you think you'll be having any tea, you can jolly well think again." The door banged hard, leaving two pairs of dejected eyes staring icily at each other and one cold heart beginning to thaw.

"I'm sorry, mate," she said quietly, her softening eyes set unwaveringly on the young boy; her conscience and mixed thoughts fighting a raging war, finally allowing her conscience to win. She patted the bed encouragingly. "Come and sit next to me, Peter."

He obeyed.

They sat for long minutes, still and quiet; two islands immersed in a shared troubled, raging sea of anxieties. Taking a deep breath she announced, "We are kind of connected by the same man, Peter." Her eyes took in his rigidly still torso, his hands clasped tightly together on his lap, his eyes far—far away, as if he was in a different world of long ago. What did he see? She wondered. Hope—despair—broken dreams and promises, or did he see what she had once seen happy, long ago days of endless sunshine, fulfilled promises and adventures; a happy family and a stable, secure home? Had his dreams been trampled upon and broken into a thousand fragments, as hers had been? Had his young life been destroyed forever too? Looking at his blank face, she wondered if her stark revelation had registered in his young mind.

Opening her mouth to repeat her statement, she closed it abruptly as he turned his innocent face towards her; inadvertently throwing a sharp stab of excruciating sadness through her sorrowful heart, making her forcibly stifle a gasp as he threw his arms around her and sobbed into her chest, "Don't leave me, Sally; please don't ever leave me," he repeated over and over again; his words jagged and full of pain, like his heart. Abruptly, he withdrew himself from her warm body, his watery eyes focused directly on Sally. "How do you know all this?"

"Auntie Rose told me."

And with those words came a grain of comfort and a shedload of questions, which were never answered, but which continually niggled and haunted him and at the forefront was always Emily, his mother.

One question loomed larger than the rest. Why hadn't his mummy come back for him? It grew like a malignant cancer and became his mantra and the cause of all his pain. Even Batman, he concluded dismally, could not answer that question; the question without an answer; the question which had made him hollow and icy cold inside, a feeling he was quickly becoming accustomed to. A slither of a smile slid onto his wan face. At least he had Sally, he told himself reassuringly over and over again.

On a dull, cold, rainy morning the rare knock on the door brought with it a rare hope in his heart. Could it be his mummy? His fast-beating heart pounded in wild anticipation.

The door opened. The voice on the other side of the door subdued the rapid beating of his heart. It was not Mummy; it was never going to be Mummy. He closed his eyes.

His eyes dropped to his right hand where, instead of his usual school lunch box was a small, battered suitcase and standing ramrod straight by his side was Auntie Rose. "Be good, Peter," she stated coldly, planting an equally icy peck on his cheek.

Puzzled eyes darted from Auntie Rose to the stranger at the door; his eyes lingering on the visitor's warm smile and rising to her friendly eyes before they looked back at a stern, stony face. "Where am I going, Auntie Rose?"

"Be good," she reiterated, before exchanging a few words with the caller, after which Peter was escorted out the door.

"Where am I going? Where's Sally? Where am I going?" Erratically, his eyes darted around trying to espy Sally but the girl was nowhere in sight.

Another long drive in another unfamiliar car brought him to another unfamiliar door, as a thousand jumbled-up thoughts rampaged through his fuddled head, and at the very core of them all, was the image of his mother. His heart raced.

His eyes wandered around the spacious, neat room and rested on a plump, kind-looking face. "Hello, Peter." The rotund lady extended her plump hand.

Protocol directives, during his brief residency at the exclusive boarding school, kicked in propelling him to extend his hand and force a smile. "Hello," he said, feeling a multitude of butterflies fluttering in his stomach, whilst his eyes once again travelled around the room taking in the stereo in one corner, a television set in another and a table set under a bay window, displaying a beautifully embroidered tablecloth, on which rested a white vase containing golden-brown chrysanthemums. A smile danced on his lips, as the comforting smell of some sort of meat pie drifted in through the kitchen. It was, he thought, all so very lovely and cosy, just like a real home. If only mummy was here.

"Hello, Peter," a deep voice boomed, making the young lad turn around to a robust man with a cheery smile. "Welcome to your new home."

... Your new home...your new home...your new home... The words echoed in Peter's head. But, where was Mummy? Where was Malcolm? Where was Sally? Who was this man? What did he mean, it was his new home? He wanted to scream the questions out. Instead, he stood ramrod straight; his small, battered suitcase clutched tightly in his hand and the butterflies in his tummy still dancing for England, as the alluring aroma of home cooking filled his nostrils, making his tummy rumble; his big, green eyes still focused on the cheerful looking man.

"Come on, Son, I'll take your case." The man lowered his hand and picked up Peter's luggage, as the boy's wary eyes took in the stranger's red cheeks, his ruffled mousy hair and his friendly encouraging smile. But you're not my daddy, he wanted to scream. I want to go home.

The following hours told him that this was his new home, at least for the time being, and these strangers were going to look after him. But, where was Mummy? Where on earth was she?

No one could, or would, answer his last question and, in time, Peter began to think less and less about her until she became a faint extraneous memory.

Peter loved his foster parents, Pauline and Kevin; he loved his new home, his room, his new school and his new friends. He was a hard-working, diligent boy who did well in all his subjects, was exceedingly good at sports and was popular. Life for the young boy was good.

From time to time, he cast a thought back to his old life which now seemed like a distant dream. Fragmented images of his mother randomly drifted into his mind, overtaken by images of Malcolm, superseded by images of Sally, Auntie Rose and Uncle Damien but on the whole, he had no time to look back; he was too busy with the present and looking forward to his future.

With a hop, skip, run and jump he travelled down the long straight road with his new best friend, Tommy; their football boots dangling over their shoulders; the top half of their torsos attired in stripy black and blue football shirts and happy smiles on their faces. They had just thrashed their rival school five goals to one and were celebrating with double-flaked ice-creams. As they turned a sharp bend at the end of the road, Peter's eyes grew in size as they gazed upon a white van, its double doors open. His heart stopped.

"Pete, what's that ambulance doing outside your house?" Tommy turned his puzzled eyes on his friend.

Peter felt his heart turn to ice; his eyes stark and wide, his feet gathering speed as faster and faster he went and nearer and larger the ominous ambulance became. His eyes dropped to the stretcher on which he saw the partly covered body of his foster mother and felt his whole world come crashing down around him, as his ice cream fell down to the ground and splattered. Mum… Mummy…

Bang—bang went the doors. Blue lights flashed. The siren screamed filling the still afternoon air with foreboding and his young heart with black dread, as he watched the vehicle speed off into the distance.

It was the longest, darkest night of Peter's young life and even Tommy's corny jokes could not summon a chuckle. Tommy's parents could do nothing to cheer the young lad up; his soft, comfy bed felt cold, hard and unyielding; the cartoons on the television screen were replaced by one stark image of Peter's foster mum on the stretcher, her face as white as a sheet, her plump body perfectly still; the blue revolving lights and the siren alert signalling to all that there was an emergency.

The spoon in his fingers went around and around the bowl, gathering up soggy flakes and dropping them back into the slush in his bowl; around and around the spoon and flakes went, like a whirling carousel; his eyes following their circular journey around their confined space; around and around and around—*knock—knock—knock*—The spoon stopped in his fingers; the milk-sodden flakes ceased their tedious journey as stark eyes darted to the closed door and one heart froze.

The door opened; words were quietly spoken. Peter watched the door close without having identified the visitor, his stark eyes following his grim-faced foster father as he pulled out a chair and sat on the opposite side of the table. The spoon and the flakes recommenced their revolving passage to nowhere and stopped their mundane dance abruptly, as Peter felt a broad hand covering his own like a warm protective glove. Slowly, he raised his eyes to his guardian's eyes and felt himself drowning in the depths of their watery wells and heard his distant echoing words. "I am sorry, Peter, Pauline, your foster mum, my wife, is dead."

Peter stared at his cold, sodden uneaten breakfast…*sorry…sorry…sorry…* The word whirled around and around in his head… *I am sorry, Peter, your mummy couldn't come; she's poorly… I am sorry, Peter, Pauline, your foster mum, my wife is dead…sorry…sorry…sorry…sorry…sorry… Sorry!* The word, he concluded, should be extinct, like the dinosaurs.

"Peter."

His foster father's gentle voice penetrated through his very heart and soul; so   gentle   and   soft;   so   hard   and   so cruel…*dead…dead…dead…sorry…sorry…sorry…dead…sorry…sorry…dead …sorry…* The irregular-sequenced words reverberated callously in his young head, making him close his eyes against his sodden, untouched food; against Kevin's mournful eyes; against the whole wide world.

Like shadows of their former selves, they existed. Pauline had selfishly and cruelly taken with her their laughter, excitement and dreams; she had stolen their passion for life; their joy; their will to live; she had scarred their hearts and souls and left them to survive in their fragile shells, leaving them numb, devoid of feeling, oblivious to others and oblivious to themselves; merely existing.

Peter's grades at school dropped; the school football team terminated his status as captain; the basketball team dumped him; his friends no longer thought he was fun or interesting and gradually, one by one, abandoned him; only one stayed true and loyal by his side, Tommy Eggleton. There was a still, silent, funereal atmosphere shrouding the house as if it too was mourning for its mistress.

Kevin sat in the kitchen, darkened considerably by the gloomy, overcast weather outside; in his hand, a glass partly filled with an amber-coloured liquid; his eyes staring starkly into the gloom; the continuous intrusive ticking of the clock on the wall invading his private thoughts. The soft *click* of the outside door made his bloodshot eyes dart in its direction, as the source of his thoughts walked sullenly in, heading directly towards the stairs and the sanctuary of his room. "Peter."

He stopped abruptly one hand on the newel, one foot poised over the first step, his eyes darting to his guardian.

"Peter, I need to talk to you."

His young heart turned to stone as he stood motionless, yearning to gallop up the stairs at top speed, bang his bedroom door against the world and bury his head under his pillow; Kevin's tone of voice told him that was not an option.

"Peter, please sit down."

His body was rigid and tensed; his eyes staring unblinkingly at a solitary crumb on the table, trying to figure out if the orange bit attached to it was marmalade, bracing himself for what was inevitably to come. He narrowed his eyes against the marmalade-laced morsel, which had seemed to be growing larger before his very eyes; he tried to close his ears against the impending words for, he knew, his foster mum's death should not have been an excuse for his rebellion against the school.

Silence cast its heavy mantle around them; heavy, thick, ominous silence which almost suffocated them in its intensity; one pair of eyes blanking out the world; the other pair firmly fixed on the glass below.

Peter heard Kevin's feet shuffle away from the table and liquid gurgling into a glass, footsteps approaching, the scraping of a chair against the hard floor and silence—an awkward cough—

Young eyes snapped open. Eyes locked. Eyes shut tight and opened wide and a young heart turned to a block of freezing ice. The words which had been spoken made Peter's young body simultaneously tremble inwardly and outwardly;

making him quiver uncontrollably and desperately will his eyes not to water, as he stared at Kevin through their blurry veils. I wasn't concentrating, his intelligent mind told him. I didn't hear him correctly.

"I am so sorry, Peter." He heard the clear voice reinstate what he thought he had misheard or misinterpreted, Kevin's additive casting the final crushing blow. "I am finding things hard to cope with on my own since Paul…"

"I'll do better at school," Peter interrupted. "I promise, I'll…"

"I am so sorry, Peter." Kevin looked directly at his charge, took a generous gulp of the amber stuff and rose once more to refill his glass. "I am truly sorry."

The young boy sat perfectly still, his glassy eyes staring into the dark unknown; the strong, pungent smell of alcohol hitting his nostrils, making him close his eyes against the brutal world he inhabited; bitter tears escaping and cascading silently down his pale, drawn face; the disgusting, raw stench of booze bringing *something* back. What *it* was, he did not know. He only knew that he had come across *it* before.

Kevin's parting words reverberated loudly and clearly in Peter's ears as, once more, he watched the ripe fields, the bustling cities and the quiet, quaint village hamlets go by… *Do well at school, Peter; that will be your foundation in life…do well at school, Peter; that will be your foundation in life…do well at school…*

As the years rolled by, so did the succession of foster homes; good, bad and indifferent. But, one thing remained stable, firm and ingrained in Peter's head; Kevin's parting words. They were locked into his body, heart, soul and mind and became the very foundation of his existence. They became his guiding force and his mantra.

After the necessary registering procedures and formalities, Peter Brooke decided to spend his first evening in the hall of residence of his university in his room, alone and with only his thoughts for company. For the very first time in his life, he was completely on his own; independent; free.

His first few hours at the university, he determined, would set the course for the rest of his life and so, while the other guys rushed down to the students' bar and started making short-term acquaintances and lifelong friends, he sat alone in his quiet room observing the scene outside his window. A smile slithered onto his lips. Already he could pick out the flirts, the chancers, the one-night standers, the easy lays, the nerds and the know-it-alls. He wondered which category he would slip into.

Life had not been a bed of roses so far. He had experienced a few happy years, followed by abandonment after abandonment. Often he had wondered what had become of his mother. Was she dead? Was she alive? Did she ever cast him a thought? For some inexplicable reason, the pungent smell of raw alcohol always brought back the memory of his mother. Still, he was here now and that's all that mattered. He would work damned hard to get to the top of the architectural ladder. A faint smile danced on his lips. He would probably ease himself in with the nerd squad, he mused.

Lying on his bed, his arms straight and motionless by his side, his ears attuned to the doors banging, sounds of laughter, footsteps retreating—growing fainter and fainter—walking away from him—walking away from the boring nerd as his mind drifted once more. Mum would have been so proud; the university was some far-off, distant place, she could only ever dream about. And yet, here he was, in spite of being abandoned, bullied, teased, rejected by so-called friends and later by girls, who thought he was an intellectual bore; mentally, sometimes physically, abused by some of his so-called guardians, laughed at by some of his peers for not wearing the latest trainers, owning the newest computer games or whatever else was in vogue. He smiled to himself saying aloud, "I am at university, on the next ring of the ladder of success." And, he could see the top.

Peter Brooke was good-looking, tall and aesthetically pleasing to the eyes with black, naturally curly hair, shrewd green eyes and a boyish look; a magnet which attracted many girls. He acknowledged them all; he had eyes for only one, Julia Foster. She was older than him; a third-year student with an easy-going, friendly nature and a warm smile; her smile reminded Peter of his mother.

One evening, on the rare occasion he ventured into the students' bar, she sidled up to him. "Hi, my name is Julia, who might you be?" She smiled.

He raised his eyes from his glass of larger and met her twinkling, brown eyes; his eyes lowering down to her warm smile. "Peter Brooke," he replied smiling back at her.

"Hi, Peter Brooke."

"Pete, please," and the casual chit-chat began. By the end of the evening, they were established friends.

In one respect, they were worlds apart, he a first-year student reading architecture, she a third-year theology student; in other aspects, they were kindred spirits opting for the quieter side of student life, placing studying above socialising and, therefore, in a category apart from the mainstream. They had lunch together, met up after lectures, studied together in the library and avidly discussed classical music. They became the best of friends and each other's confidante. Sex did not enter either mind, as both minds were directly focused on the ladder of success; sex would come into the equation later.

He glanced at his watch; six fifteen. His brow furrowed. It was not like Julia to be late. He glanced at his watch sometime later before picking up his pen. Six forty-five. Students were appearing and disappearing through the double doors with no Julia in sight. Seven o'clock. His dejected eyes rose to the closed doors and, rapidly picking up his books he stuffed them into his rucksack, hauled it over his shoulder and briskly walked out of the library.

Her door was firmly shut, and uncharacteristically, no other student was loitering about on the landing. He pounded on the door a second time. The door remained stubbornly closed; a seed of nervous tension starting to grow in Peter's head. This was so unlike Julia.

Like an iced statue he stood in the courtyard, his eyes starkly staring at the scene in front of him; figures bustling around an obscured bundle on the floor; anxious voices projected in different tones and speeds, as his eyes dropped to the bundle beneath, a sharp-bladed dagger thrusting into the very soul of his heart, as his still eyes met her open, dead eyes, which stayed with him from this day until his dying day.

He attended Julia's funeral, one among many mourners; shook hands with the grieving parents, his mouth remaining firmly shut. There was nothing to say.

Grief gave him no respite. His anguished eyes saw Julia in all things and in everybody. Julia's spirit touched his very soul as the gentle autumnal breeze touched his face; he saw the essence of her spirit in the flight of the common blackbird and her gentleness as he watched the natural flow of the meandering river. He saw and felt her everywhere and in all things. She had never left him, but she had left an inexplicable, excruciatingly painful hollow in the pit of his stomach and in the depth of his beating heart and, he knew, only one thing could provide a temporary release; a release, he remembered, his foster dad, Kevin, had succumbed to.

In the privacy of his room, he switched on an oceanic track, reached for the bottle, unscrewed the metal top, poured a generous measure into a mug and swallowed a mouthful of the potent amber liquid. Closing his eyes, he allowed his body, mind, heart and soul to drift.

The potency of the alcohol, mixed with the sounds of the mighty ocean, washed over him; his mind imagined a strong rolling surf as it came rolling in and breaking onto the shore; each single wave in the far distance giving birth to a new wave, as it had done for millions of years, and which now gave him a temporary wave of inexplicable peace.

He took another sip and closed his eyes once more and this time…*they were walking hand-in-hand along the soft white sand of a tropical, deserted beach where he stopped, took Julia into his arms and kissed her…laying her down and made love to her…* Eyes sprang wide open. Automatically, his hand brought the glass up to his lips, swilling down the remnants of the golden liquid; his head shaking from side to side. "One snag here," he said aloud to the empty glass, "I am still a goddam virgin." He laughed incredulously. He poured himself another measure, resolving to amend the matter he had just declared.

Within a week, he had lost his virginity to a second-year student he barely knew, but whose reputation everyone knew. The girl meant nothing to him; the sex, on the other hand, gave him a sense of release which, as far as he was concerned, far surpassed what the amber liquid was offering him. Sex became his medicine and his obsession.

Girls soon learned of his sexual prowess and were only too eager to have a taste for themselves. He became both a saviour and a destroyer of relationships, but never did he make a promise to anyone. Peter Brooke is what you saw; Peter Brooke is what you got; nothing more; nothing less.

He became an expert in the art of seduction, but never, ever did he deliberately set out to hurt anyone, for he knew well the rawness of pain.

He graduated from university with a first-class honours degree and an honorary degree in wooing any female he fancied and he used both qualifications to his ultimate advantage.

Rapidly he soared up the ladder of success, and simultaneously, he notched up his sexual conquests. Women of all ages, colours and creeds flocked to him; clambered to be by his side and wanted to be part of his life, hoping to be the chosen one. And so, he drifted from one to another—to another—to another.

His current girlfriend, Amy Pilkington, suited him fine for the time being. Tall, slim, her long silky tresses blonde and straight, she was a glamorous trophy on his arm and her casual attitude towards relationships, mirroring his own, was an added bonus but, just lately, her attitude seemed to be changing and she wanted more. Being the only child of a renowned surgeon, she had daddy's money to burn and she showered her current beau with expensive gifts he did not need or want; funded expensive five-star holidays to far-flung tropical destinations and gave him all the sex he wanted.

Peter Brooke felt suffocated with love, which he knew, was false and unreal; bought love.

They continued to be a unit, and while she built sandcastles in the sky, he bedded hordes of women behind her back and thoroughly enjoyed the diversion whilst, at the same time, his business rapidly grew, thanks to Amy Pilkington's daddy.

Amy's loyalty throughout the years peaked and waned, as she created diversions of her own with a fling here, a casual affair there; still, she stuck with Peter and his baggage.

Years Later

He placed one heavy foot in front of the other, both feet feeling like two blocks of concrete; his heart a stone; his head whirling with an assortment of nightmarish scenarios and, a few seconds later, no scenario at all; his eyes staring directly ahead and seeing nothing but a stark coffin; his coffin.

He sat rigid at the kitchen table unseeing and unyielding, a heavy blanket of numbness overtaking all his senses, as he sat and stared into nothingness itself.

The bark of a dog made him blink and slip back into the present and jump forward into his dismal future and back into the here and now; into himself and into a body which was slowly, but surely, releasing its grip on the world. Very gradually, he began to formulate a string of thoughts; one thought loomed large; cancer.

Closing his eyes, he willed the calm to descend on him; the proverbial calm before the raging storm played complete havoc with his body, heart, mind and soul. Fervently, he willed to obliterate everything and everybody from his mind and to breathe in only the here and now; to think of the here and now and to banish thoughts about the inevitable grizzly end; to feel and revel in Peter Brooke and not to walk in the shadow of death. But, as he began to immerse himself in the present, uninvited images crashed into his mind, bringing with them memories he had long ago banned from entering, and with them came pain.

Staring starkly into the past, he felt the familiar tug in his heart; the twisted gnawing in his guts; the fear, despondency, childhood innocence, raw betrayal, deceit and the last time he saw his beloved mother. Only it wasn't his mother but some unfortunate soul in a long, tattered skirt, a stained jumper, her grey-black hair long and straggly, her eyes staring into oblivion, her body shaking uncontrollably as she shuffled about from place to place. Drugs and alcohol were blamed for her downfall. He knew otherwise. He knew Malcolm Mosterby was her slow, silent killer, just as cancer was his slow, silent killer.

Malcolm, the ruination of dreams and the destroyer of futures; Malcolm, his inadvertent inspiration, because without Malcolm, there would never have been a successful Peter Brooke for, in the aftermath of having attempted to destroy the boy, he made him the man he became; conscientious and confident; a success.

Inadvertently, Malcolm Moserby had also moulded him into a materialistic, self-seeking womaniser and into the lonely man he now was.

"Malcolm," he said his name aloud for the first time in years; his name on his tongue made the image in his eyes more alive, more real. "Malcolm," he stated a second time; the man who had cheated on his partner, Emily; the man who had abandoned his own step-children; a man who had abandoned him on the rough wild sea of independence and left him to sink or swim. His mind drifted to the last time he had seen his guardian at the exclusive school... It was the day of the Christmas concert. Excitement was in the air. Mums and Dads were arriving. What joy! And then, the grim conversation in that small gloomy room... *Your mummy is not well Peter...she is very ill...* Malcolm could have made her well; he could have saved her if he really wanted to.

Instead, he threw her out of the house and into a poky flat, and soon after, withdrew his funding from the exclusive boys' boarding school, leaving his former partner and her child to fend for themselves. If only alcohol hadn't already got its destructive tentacles into Mum, he thought; if only it hadn't sucked the energy and will to fight; if only—And, the spiral downwards was, oh, so very swift once social services were involved and shifted him from one foster home and into another while his childhood, together with his innocence, disappeared into obscurity; never to be regained; his resolve, on the other hand, grew stronger by the day. He would survive...

He lowered his resigned eyes to his clasped hands resting on the table. And now, he concluded, he would not survive, cancer would see to that. Closing his heavy, lustreless eyes he sighed deeply accepting the fate the gods had pronounced on him. Now, he told himself, he had to make amends, before it was too late.

The first rays of the morning light filtered through the curtains, bringing with them a sense of purpose, urgency and determination, for there was much to be done and not a single second to waste.

After a light breakfast of poached egg on toast, orange juice and coffee, for these were as much as he could stomach these days, he set his mind to work. Opening the smooth top of his expensive fountain pen, a present from Amy, he opened his writing pad and scribed a list of names, one after the other, in big, bold, capital letters:

SARAH
EMMA
JADE AND TRACY
MEREDITH
MARY
AMY
TOMMY

His eyes scanned and rescanned the list of names, the images of the people named looming alternatively in his head.

Note after note, he meticulously scribed and every single word in each sentence he carefully read, mulled over and reread several times more; every single sentence his eyes carefully scrutinised; each word memorised; each woman remembered until words, sentences, images swam erratically in his head, weaving in and out of each other; mingling and intermingling; linking and interlinking until they all merged together into one blurry mass and he was firmly implanted in the centre; in the eye of the fuzzy storm.

Rising, he moved his decrepit torso to the vast, plush corner sofa and sat in the very centre, allowing his dying body to sink and mould into the subtle leather, as it cushioned him giving him a grain of comfort. Closing his eyes, images crashed into his head. One by one, like obedient soldiers, they marched in; each one demanding his full, undivided attention; each one silently pleading to be exclusively addressed with the respect it never previously got. Sarah took centre stage, making his heart tighten.

She was different to the others, he mused; her image becoming clearer by the second, and the more clearer she became in his mind's eye, the more poignant became her deceit. Sarah, the girl who had blushed profusely at the sight of a male stripper, like a timid bird, becoming the ravenous vulture who had savagely ripped out a part of him and devoured it for her own ends for he was, he concluded, only the ends to her means.

Snapping starkly open, his eyes relived the scenes which led to her ultimate betrayal…the encounter in the pub—the wedding—bumping into each other in the hospital grounds—the deal—the… His eyes slammed shut, unable to relive the scene that followed, but the scene of betrayal and deceit ruthlessly invaded without an invitation and fought for its place in his reflections, before they too would be obliterated forever.

A violent surge of bitterness washed over him, followed by another treacherous one and another and, like a mighty ocean, one surge overlapped another—then another—then another until he felt himself submerged in its destructive waters.

Opening his mouth, he tipped the remnants of his drink inside and poured himself another. The liquid trickled down his throat; down—down—down it slithered into the pit of his stomach; easing, comforting; camouflaging reality with its soft, hazy blanket; softening Sarah's deceitful eyes and her lying mouth. Sarah, who took a precious part of him and gave him back not a morsel in return; Sarah, the woman who almost succeeded in snatching from him an invaluable, precious gift of dying with dignity and peace; almost, but not quite, because *someone* had saved him from drowning in despair; *someone* had come to his rescue when he had almost lost everything, including himself; *someone* he could rely on to be with him at the very end and to give him the peace and dignity that was rightfully his.

Rising he strode to the sideboard and pulled out a drawer, his fingers extracting a small velvet box. Opening the lid, his eyes looked down at the gleaming gold heart fastened onto an expensive chain, a small smile breaking out on his lips. It died a sudden death. Locating Sarah would be a problem; he'd heard she'd moved several times and where she was based now, nobody seemed to know, or care.

It became his mission; a venture in which time was of the essence because it was time that was running out—fast. So, with no precious time to lose, he forced down the last piece of toast, touched with only a touch of spread, and started out on his lonely quest.

Standing rigidly outside a scuffed green-painted door, his heart pounding wildly, he unclamped his tightly clenched fingers and knocked. Seconds later it opened. The gasp did not come from his mouth.

"P… Peter."

"Yep; it's me," he responded in as cheerful voice as he could fake; while she stared back at him in a total state of incredulity, as his mouth opened and his vituperate words spewed out. "Or, rather, it's my cancer you are so rudely staring at." He enunciated each word clearly, deliberately, aiming to achieve maximum effect, secretly squirming at the audacity of his caustic additive.

"Oh, Peter—P… Peter, I am so very sorry."

"I am not sorry. Stop gawping, Julie."

"I'm sorry."

"Stop apologising."

"I'm sorry."

He stared at her plump face, his eyes lowering to her frumpy skirt, thinking back to the glamorous bride he remembered. Marriage, he thought, certainly hadn't done her looks any good. Sharply, he brought himself back to the present. "I need to get in contact with Sarah," he stated, watching her shake her head from side to side.

"I am sorry, Peter. I have lost all contact with Sarah. She moved away to another town, that's all I know." She stared at his disappointed face, ravaged by the effects of his devastating illness; his sunken eyes and pinched cheeks; taking in the paleness of his complexion.

So the happy little family had moved to a place where he could not find them. Turning abruptly, his ears registered the *click* of the door as he walked despondently away, oblivious to the fact that it had reopened a few seconds later.

"Wait…wait, Peter, I have an address."

His exhausted feet walked down a long row of terraced houses and finally stopped, his fists banging on the door, his feet tapping a nervous rhythm on the wet pavement, his focused eyes glued to the closed door.

Finally, after long, torturous seconds the door opened and Peter's eyes stared into the eyes of a stranger. "Does Sarah live here?" His hopeful eyes remained fixed on the man at the door, thinking how uncouth and unfriendly he looked, wondering who the heck he was. Seconds of laden silence was broken by a guttural grunt and the sight of the door closing. "Please, I am dying. I need to know."

The door opened. The man withdrew into the bowels of the house, where a figure hunched at a table was engrossed in homework.

"My son," grunted the man.

"Sarah's son?" The rhetorical question escaped Peter's mouth before he could rein it in. He followed the burly man into another room and the door closed. Within half an hour, the two complete strangers knew everything they needed to know about each other.

"I am truly sorry, mate." Brian's eyes looked into the eyes of the dying man, where he saw his own miserable reflection.

Minutes ticked away as both men reflected on each other's dismal fate and the part Sarah had played in both of their lives. Peter broke the heavy silence.

"Do you have an address?" His heart sank as he saw Brian's head shake from side to side, but his following words lifted his sinking heart.

"But, I do have her sister's address."

Peter's skeletal fingers dived in and rummaged in the depths of his coat pocket. "Brian, when my daughter is thirteen, could you make sure she gets this?" He opened the lid of the velvet box, his eyes looking up to see a tinge of a smile appear on Brian's lips.

"Of course, mate, I shall make it my personal mission."

With a lighter heart, Peter walked out of the house.

He went to bed that night with a soul lifted from part of its burden. The velvet box with its precious contents had been safely deposited; a sealed envelope, addressed to his daughter, was propped up on the mantelpiece and Peter's heart was beating with a steady, satisfied rhythm.

The healthy deciduous cherry tree gave Peter shade, solace and inexplicable calm as he sat beneath its sturdy branches; the delicate pink blossoms touching his skeletal arms, which were devoid of the taut muscles they once sported; the light, warm breeze gently rustling the leaves, lulling his mind back to happier times, when his thoughts were not preoccupied with images of coffins, last will and testaments, stern-faced consultants, stark and sterile rooms and grim death-beds, but were preoccupied with planning the next move on the next girl and how he was going to entice her into bed. His thoughts rested on one girl, who had replaced him with a dog; a dog he had given to her, in the hope of securing her everlasting love and loyalty.

Emma, he mused, the woman who had hurtled into his life, who was as bold as brass and as big a flirt as they came. Closing his eyes, he savoured the warmth of the spring sunshine on his face; his thoughts drifting further, a smile creeping onto his lips. Yes, she was a confirmed flirt, rather like himself back in the day. His smile grew and vanished. "But, she was a tease," he said aloud, "and for that, she had to pay the price."

She paid. He nodded his head. In more ways than one, not only did he take Fluffball away from her, he denied her any access stating determinedly, "If she doesn't want me, then she can't have Fluffball."

Now in the cold light of day, as death was determinedly marching towards him, his mind was changing course and regrets seeped in. It had been a cruel, contemptible thing to do. Whichever way you looked at it, his pooch-napping of Fluffball was vile and unnecessary. And now, he determined, she was going to get him back; perhaps, not in the way she'd like but she was going to get him back. And so he started to formulate a plan.

The task would be heart-breaking. He assessed the situation as he rose from his wicker chair and headed for the conservatory door. The last thing he wanted was to let Fluffball go, but it had to be done; it was time to set the wheels in motion.

Carefully he withdrew a receptacle and placed Fluffball's cute photo on the table before the urn. "It's almost time for you to go, my friend," he said softly before opening the lid and taking one final look.

His drifting mind floated from this girl to that; many didn't get a look-in, they'd long been forgotten; some made his dying heart twinge and some made his heart cringe.

Tracy and Jade; he shook his head, his lips forming into a smile of regret. Because of his own devious behaviour, he ended up abandoned by both. But, he reflected, they had both taught him a lesson he would take to his grave. A true friendship was a friendship to the very end, no matter how many unsavoury ordeals it had thrown its way. He closed his tired eyes, desperately fighting off the urge to succumb to sleep, his mind drifting once more, his heart-crushing with guilt as Meredith and Tommy came into sharp focus. The guilt in his heart grew and shrouded him with an unforgiving blanket. Unable to take any more, he rose to his feet and rushed towards the drinks cabinet, his impatient fingers unscrewing the metal top, his mind urging the potent liquid to quickly pour out into his glass and down his throat; down into his guilty gullet; into his guilty stomach and numb all his guilt; to kill it so that he would be prevented from thinking, remembering, regretting; wishing the potency of the fiery substance to kill his heart, body and soul; wishing it could kill him; dead—dead—Dead!

The burning substance failed to obey his command; instead, it enhanced his fears, his guilt and the black devious image of himself, enhancing his historically evil ways; the cunning tricks he used to get girls into bed; the relationships he destroyed for his own selfish means; the hearts and dreams he broke, not to mention, the futures he demolished without a second thought. It was all as clear as day, his eyes seeing the devil himself; the devil that was Peter Brooke. And for what? He now asked himself. A laborious sigh rippled jaggedly through him; for a bit of action; for a bit of skirt; a quick fuck; for minutes of pleasure before he swiftly moved on to the next victim and the next and the next. And out of the hundreds he had conquered, how many did he remember? Ten—fifteen at a push, he answered himself honestly. And, had it all been worth it? The voice of conscience asked. He squeezed his eyes tightly not wanting, able daring to answer. Quickly, he replenished his empty glass and drank himself into a stupor.

The first rays of light steeled into his lounge where he lay fully clothed on the sofa, an empty bottle tossed aside on the plush carpet beneath him, his aching heart pounding for England, his skeletal form as stiff as a corpse and his mind coiled into a fuzzy blur. *Tap—tap—tap—*The unobtrusive, successive knocking alerted his red-rimmed eyes to the door and his body to heave heavily; visitors were the very last thing he wanted.

But this one particular visitor was not calling on Peter because she was a dear, loyal friend; the woman was being paid for her services.

Closing his eyes on the opening door, he sank back into his well of misery; a place which, inexplicably, brought him dark comfort.

"Hi, Pete; how are we today?" The unwanted intruder chirped cheerfully, seemingly oblivious to the heavy silence permeating the room, as she cast her observant eyes on her hung-over patient, seeing everything and rapidly sequencing and assessing the turn of events, which had led to the empty bottles and a scattering of crisps on the floor; her eyes turning back to the dishevelled figure on the sofa; her heart-tugging for this abandoned dying man. Dying but not dead yet, her professional voice stated, setting her hands to work as they started to clear up Peter's mess.

The disparaging frown he threw her way did not put Gail off; she'd seen it all and had heard all the negative comments; her hide was thick.

"Think about it, Peter," she said softly, as she placed a fresh mug of coffee onto the coffee table before him, knowing that the suggestion she tossed over to him was hard for him to digest.

"It's absurd," he stated, throwing her a caustic look. "I won't even be here in six months' time, anyway, what's the point?"

Her hands akimbo; her small, kind eyes looked down on him. "Maybe, but you are here now and your quality of life matters; do you really want to be remembered as a drunk, Peter?" The small green pebbles peeping out from a podgy face bore into the very depths of his soul.

Nothing more was said on the matter. The tidying of the house was completed; Peter's medical requirements were adhered to and the door closed behind Gail, leaving Peter to reside alone in his self-made well of inner misery.

Despair, negativity, gloom and despondency were not obliging friends; neither were they helpful in assessing the benefits of AA meetings, which flashed in and out of his mind, making him question his own sanity… *Think about it, Peter…* Gail's words floated annoyingly around in his head, mixed with distorted images of recovering drunks sitting in a circle, relating to each other their sad stories resulting from regretful life choices. "I am not an alcoholic," he stated loudly to the four walls around him; walls which could not contradict his statement. *Oh yes you are,* came the resounding contradiction from the voice of reason. I am dying; what the fuck do I need an AA meeting for? *Maybe you are dying, but you are here now and the quality of life matters …the quality of life matters…the quality of life matters…* Like a song pressed on repeat, the words echoed repeatedly in his head, each word becoming louder and clearer; demanding to be heard and, more importantly, to be obeyed. "The quality of life matters," he said aloud.

One heavy foot in front of the other brought him to the double glass doors and, pushing through them, his ears were instantly bombarded with a motley gathering of voices. Turning back, his hand reaching for the door, his feet ready to run, he felt the slightest touch on his arm. "Come in—come in," a friendly voice encouraged. "I'm Terry."

Peter cast his derisive eyes on the man standing before him, his guts wrenching and twisting as a sickly lump rose and lodged stubbornly in his parched throat, his feet eager to run.

"Please come in," Terry signalled to the crowd within. "We don't bite."

Sitting rigidly in the large circle, Peter's eyes dared to glance cautiously around the unfamiliar surroundings, feeling as if he was the intruder on the show; a gate-crasher who had inadvertently stumbled into a place where he did not wish to stay; his green suspicious eyes flitting from a dishevelled looking middle-aged man, to a pristinely attired character, to a girl barely out of her teens and on to a grey-haired woman, who looked well past her seventies. Again the urge to run swept over him like a mighty tsunami; to run to the nearest off-licence and grab a bottle of the strongest stuff the shop sold; anything that would disperse his pain.

"Hello everyone, my name is Judy and I am an alcoholic."

"Hi," they all responded in varying degrees of enthusiasm, while her stark admission cut sharply through Peter's consciousness, forcing his involuntary eyes to look at the speaker and scrutinise her intently. She can't be an alcoholic, his eyes told him as they surveyed her carefully applied make-up, her shoulder-length, silky hair and her well-cut designer suit. His eyes shot up to her eyes, serious and sober; her clear, concise words telling him she was clean; his ears listening intently to her life story and then to another, following a person's account with his continual temptations; after which, the leader stood up, about to bring the meeting to an end with the Serenity Prayer. A soft voice spoke, "May I speak, please?"

"Of course," nodded the leader smiling genially as he politely sat back down.

Peter's eyes drifted to the smartly dressed woman, who chose to stand to address her audience; his mind telling him he'd had enough of this outpouring of souls; his contained silence silently shouting at her to make it snappy; he needed a drink.

Half-listening, and silently urging her to hurry up and say what she needed to get off her chest so that he could get the hell out of the place; his eyes desperately willed her to speed up but as he stared at the smartly dressed female, a strange feeling of—of—*something* he could not pinpoint invaded him.

Abruptly rising like a Jack-in-the-box, the chair falling with a loud *thud* behind him, he muttered, "I'm sorry, I have to go," and fled out of the hall and out of the building into the fresh, cool, calming air away from the drunks; away from their desperate self-inflicted consequences, resulting from their decisions, and into the nearest off-licence.

Half an hour later, a generous measure of neat brandy in his glass, he brought the glass up to his lips and gulped a mouthful, feeling the potent liquid slowly slither down his throat and into his gullet; gasping as he felt the rawness of alcohol fighting a war with his guts, which were already being ravaged by an aggressive tumour.

Closing his tired eyes, he willed the hoard of women, whom he had bedded, to accompany his thoughts and take him to a happier place. Instead, one solitary female invaded his mind and stayed with him; her voice penetrating his heart, body and soul; her name echoing again and again and again and again… *Emily… Emily… Emily…* He brought the glass up to his lips and took another swig and another until blessed oblivion took him for its own.

Gail found him fully dressed, with only one empty bottle to clear away. "I went." She heard the two words exuded from his parched mouth and smiled victoriously to herself, knowing exactly what he was referring to.

"Will you be going to another meeting?" She enquired casually sometime later, as she set a plate of buttered toast and a coffee before him. She did not receive an answer.

The name haunted him throughout the day as he attempted to read the papers, watch television and go through some papers relating to work; filtering in and lingering in his mind and making its home there—*Emily—Emily—Emily*, for that was the name of the smartly-attired woman at the AA meeting; the recovering alcoholic's name—his mother's name. He closed his eyes, his mother's warm smile burning through the darkness; green, intelligent eyes focused on him; her hair now sprinkled with grey, but once so dark—so soft. "Mummy." Her name was but a whisper on his lips. Another image crashed into his head; Malcolm, the destroyer. His eyes shot open, stark and alert; his dying guts wrenching with a vengeance. Draining the remnants of his drink, he willed her image to disappear.

... Hello, I am Emily and I am an alcoholic... The words reverberated loudly in his swimming head, laced heavily with distorted images of Malcolm—Saint Bartholemew's—secret notes to Batman—the exclusive boarding school—the Christmas performance—his mum's absence—his swift exit from the boarding school—Auntie Rose and Uncle Damian and dear, dear Sally—A smile flickered on his lips and widened as images of Pauline and Kevin filtered in; his smile rapidly dying as Tommy's words crashed into his exhausted head... *Pete, what's that ambulance doing outside your house...* He had known there and then that tragedy had struck and bitter heartache would surely follow and stay with him forever... *I am sorry, Peter, Pauline, your foster mum, my wife, is dead...dead...dead... Dead!* ... Like he himself would be soon; dead as a doornail; dead as a post; dead as dead can be; Dead!

Her warm motherly face suffused his senses; her voice so sweet, so comforting; her smile warm and friendly; the faint smell of lilac about her; her touch so soft and gentle, as she bandaged the graze on his knee; her comforting hugs. She was his *mum*; his mum and no one else's.

The stranger at the meeting loomed into his mind once more, making his head shake vigorously from side to side. How could he even contemplate such an absurd notion? He continued to shake his head. But—but—there was *something* about her; it was that voice so soft and gentle. It was his mum's voice; only his mum could have that soothing voice. Abruptly he rose. Swiftly replenishing his glass, he swilled the golden liquid down in one go. Still, her image loomed.

Involuntarily, his feet walked on and on until they reached their unwilling destination. Pushing the door open, he walked in and sat down, his wary eyes watching as the hall gradually filled up with a motley gathering of recovering alcoholics; his eyes darting this way and that until they rested on Emily who, oblivious to his interest in her, engaged herself in conversation with a fellow recovering AA member. The years rolled back as he began to make associations in his head. The way the woman placed one hand on top of the other and placed both on her lap; the way she inclined her head to one side as she smiled; her eyes; her mouth; her skin; mature in years now but all reminiscent of his mother.

Could it be? He asked himself, his heart thudding with the mere possibility. No, he severely told himself. His mum would not be seen dead in one of these places. And yet—and yet—His swimming mind whirled. And yet—there had been the distinctive smell of raw alcohol on her breath on more than one occasion, he recalled. Did she have a problem all those years ago? No—no, he swiftly answered his own gnawing question—and yet—that raw smell; the salient raw smell of potent, neat alcohol. He never forgot it. He would carry it with him to his grave. His eyes turned away from her, unable to meet her eyes should they clash with his; his thundering heart breaking into a thousand fragments, each fragment silently asking, *Are you my mum?*

She cast him furtive glances, careful not to attract his attention, cautious not to jump to any wild conclusions, avoiding the trap of assuming or presuming; careful to act her normal, cautious self. But, there was *something* about this newcomer; *something* uncanny; *something* that made her heart slice in two with sheer raw pain; *something* which made her think.

She shook her head as her eyes watched him, her ears oblivious to every single word the speaker was saying. A mere coincidence, she told herself firmly, and yet—and yet—the curly hair, the green eyes but—but this fellow, she thought, is so thin; so ill-looking; it could not possibly be Peter. It cannot be Peter, she told herself over and over again.

Their eyes clashed and simultaneously dived into a mutual world for a few brief seconds, before focusing on the present, the recovering alcoholics around them and their shared sad, but all too real, testimonies. Soft tentacles stealthily crept around their thoughts and wove memories of long ago; memories which had been dead and buried and had now been resurrected.

Standing close, yet poles apart, they waited for their hot drinks to be poured out the urn; two hearts aware of each other's presence; two pairs of feet urging to run in opposite directions, yet desperately willing to stay put; two pairs of eyes solidly focused on the hot black liquid as it was poured into their respective cups.

The meeting ended. The recovering alcoholics dispersed to see another day, or drink another secretive drink; some walking out with a renewed spirit of hope; others as despondent as when they had walked into the meeting.

God grant me the serenity… The closing prayer of the meeting echoed loudly and repeatedly in Emily's head. Serenity, however, remained an elusive friend as an old, uninvited, unwanted, destructive friend crashed in and grew in her head; a companion she could not wish away no matter how fervently she tried and, the more she closed her eyes to its image, the larger, clearer and alluring the image became making her heart race, her guts wrench and twist and her eyes shoot towards the place where her *friend* resided; her feet swiftly following; her trembling fingers pulling open the door; her impatient fingers digging deep— deeper; stretching; touching her treasure which had rested untouched, but never forgotten, for decades.

The cool, smooth touch of the glass made her fingers abruptly withdraw as if she had touched a piece of burning coal; her heart beat faster, racing uncontrollably as a herd of memories rushed before her eyes—Malcolm's twisted, accusing face—vomit rising to her throat, spilling out her mouth on to the plush carpet—her drunken, dishevelled, unwashed body sprawled out on the bed like a piece of trash—Peter—

Frantically, her shaky fingers snatched the bottle and pulled it away from the piles of books, magazines, a sowing box and long-forgotten, unopened boxes of chocolates. Sitting rigidly on the sofa, her unblinking eyes stared at her old friend—an enemy—friend—an enemy—She couldn't decide which and while she stared, the clock continued to tick away the remnants of her sobriety and time, like the layers of an onion, peeling away layer by layer, day by day, month by month, year by year, until she arrived where she needed to be. The raw, unquenchable pain deep—deep down within her propelled her fingers to unscrew the metal top and pour the stuff into a glass.

Eyes stared at the golden liquid; inviting, welcoming, alluring and bringing the glass up to her mouth, an image cashed into her head—his twinkling eyes and black, curly, unruly hair; his engaging smile dissipating her urge to take the first fatal drink. The image grew; one minute he was kicking his football about; the next he was sauntering down the road with his friend. She closed her eyes. What was his name? Jimmy—no—no—Billy; yes, Billy Moffatt and for a moment, she wondered what had happened to him, a jar of tadpoles appearing in the scene making her smile. The smile vanished as buried words resurrected from the dead...

We have found a fantastic school for you, Peter... Malcolm's words boomed loudly in her head. It was the beginning of the end... *Enjoy your tad-poling, Peter...* Malcolm's words reverberated loud and clear, as fresh memories overtook and burned savagely inside her skull—The expensive exclusive boarding school—the Christmas concert Malcolm banned her from attending—her first bottle which Joyce Cummings had handed over to her; she never did pay her back—Peter's special friend and confidante, Batman—A sharp iced blade pierced her gnawing heart, making her trembling fingers curl around the glass.

She felt the liquid slide down her throat, making her inwardly scream, *I should have been your confidante, son. It should have been me—Me! Not a fictitious character in a cape and mask in some comic or film. It should have been me!* She took another generous mouthful of the raw, burning liquid and another and another until the small room, and all it contained, became hazy as if belonging in a different world. Another mouthful and another until her guts stopped their ferocious gnawing, wrenching, writhing and twisting; another and another mouthful until her fast-beating heart stopped racing; another and another mouthful until the pain evaporated and everything around her took on a rosy glow and serenity, at last, entered her tortured soul.

The night was long and torturous and gave Peter no peace, as he tossed and turned and made endless mugs of tea; two images stuck stubbornly in his mind, fighting a raging war with each other and with his wavering willpower.

She had not left him since her identity came to light, her image firmly establishing itself in his head, bringing long-forgotten memories to the forefront. These memories, he now determined, needed to be addressed. Time was not on his side.

Her softly-spoken words, her mannerisms; the fact that she was in an AA meeting told him he had encountered Emily, his mother. That certainty was firmly planted in his mind, but did the way she had looked at him with those soft, warm eyes tell him that she had recognised him? His eyes dropped to the liquid in his glass. What to do now? He shook his head from side to side. What on earth should he do now? He asked himself over and over again, as a host of memories in his fuzzy head vied for his attention. One thought gained special attention; his mother's love for him; if only it hadn't been marred by Malcolm's presence. He snapped his eyes shut to obliterate his guardian's image; closed his ears to his damning words. If only it wasn't for the bastard.

The liquid in the glass remained untouched; the bottle loomed warm and inviting as a little voice in his head whispered. *What have you got to lose, Peter, you're dying anyway.* The voice grew in volume. *What have you got to lose, Brooke, your liver is good for no one… What have you got to lose?* His temptress shouted. *What have you got to lose?* The splintered shards of the exploded bomb in his head, invaded every tiny crevice of his conscious mind, repeating over and over again… *What have you got to lose, Brooke, you're a dead man walking.*

The strangled words squeezed forcibly out of his mouth. "My integrity." And, with the last word dying softly on his lips, a calmness, like a soothing wave, gently washed over him. Serenity had stealthily entered his soul.

His expectant eyes roamed around the large hall and watched as the familiar figures made casual conversation with each other; waiting expectantly for one particular person to occupy a chair. It remained unoccupied; one recovering alcoholic had not turned up; one heart began to deflate as the door opened no more and the leader of the group called his fellow recovering alcoholics together. The meeting commenced and so did the sad stories. Not one word filtered through Peter's consciousness. He continued to stare at the empty chair; his mind whirling, wondering.

A new recovering alcoholic occupied the chair at the next meeting. Peter smiled at the attractive woman, his heart hurting.

Emily invaded every waking moment. Why wasn't she attending the meetings? Had she succumbed? Was her absence a secret sign, telling him that she had recognised him and wanted nothing to do with him?

Tentative enquiries informed him that she had had a slip. Her sponsor would tell him no more, no matter how much he pressed, leaving him to wonder and worry.

It became his ultimate passion; to find his mother; to help her before it was too late for the both of them. Time was of the essence; time was fast running out. Soon there would be no time.

Eventually, his persistent enquiries and stalwart determination bore fruit.

His stomach churning, clenched fists by his side, he stood waiting with bated breath for the door to open.

What he saw he remembered to his dying day.

His eyes adjusted to the dimly lit room and drifted to the frail woman lying perfectly still on a bed. The woman he beheld was his mother; the mother of whom he had been robbed; the mother who had been so warm, so gentle; his beloved mother who was dying before his own dying eyes. Alcohol had seen to that.

He felt the beat of his racing heart and counted—one—two—three—four—five—six—seven—How many more beats did he have left? He wondered. How many more beats would his mother's heart make? Whose heart would stop first? Who was going to mourn for whom?

Step by slow solitary step, he forced his leaden feet to propel forwards—third step—fourth step—nearer and nearer until both feet stopped, his heart stopping in unison; wishing it would never restart so that he would not be forced into mourning for this woman; his mother.

"Say what you need to say, Peter," a soft voice urged for Jasmine, Emily's sponsor, knew the signs well.

Peter heard the door *click* softly. Heavy silence shrouded mother and son, making him feel as if he was already ensconced in his lonely casket. *Tick-tick-tick…* The clock in his head ticked away the ominous minutes. *Tick-tick-tick…* Time was running out. *Tick-tick…*

Cautiously, as if he was handling a rare invaluable jewel, he picked up his mother's warm hand and covered it with his own skeletal hand, a hundred or more pins pricking viciously at his heart and all the while the clock was ticking—*tick-tick-tick-tick-tick*—reverberating loudly in his head, invading all his senses. *Tick-tick-tick*—Hurry up before it's too late, it seemed to say.

Opening his parched lips, he found his mouth was as dry and grainy as the desert sand. Squeezing his eyes tightly, he willed with all of his might for the appropriate words to squeeze out his mouth and to filter through and permeate the depths of this dying woman's heart. Tighter and tighter, he pressed his eyes together, four words surging out of his mouth. "I love you, Mummy." He opened his eyes to her open, still, stark eyes.

The bustle outside the door made him release his hand from her hand and turn his glassy eyes on the opening door, his heart flipping, his stomach somersaulting. "Sally!" He gasped. "Oh my God, Sally!"

Eyes wide as saucers he stared unblinkingly at the flustered woman before him, who roughly pushed past him and fell onto the bed, lifting and embracing Emily tightly as she sobbed, her whole body heaving, her heart-rending sobs filling the bleak room with a blanket of excruciating sadness, while the warmth seeped out of Emily's still, silent, dead body.

Peter looked on, his whole body numb, apart from his confused brain cells, which were trying desperately to make a connection between his mother and Sally. They failed.

Tick—tick—tick—The infuriating clock continued to measure time, but now it was of no consequence; one life was already extinguished. *Tick—tick—tick*— Not long now before time ended another. *Tick—tick—tick*—

Slumping down on a high-backed chair, he buried his head in his skinny hands, his ears finely attuned to the heart-breaking, heaving sobs while inwardly he felt numb, cheated; already dead and buried.

Minutes seemed to turn into hours; hours into days and yet barely ten minutes had passed. Emily, his mother, had not been a part of this world for ten minutes, he reflected, and already it had seemed like an eternity. So many years wasted, lost and never to be reclaimed; so many tragic years that could have been filled with joy, perhaps with grandchildren and a daughter-in-law for mum to fuss over; so many dark, wasted, empty years; a mother without a son; a son without his mother; empty and now dead and beyond redemption.

The soft tap on his shoulder made his whole body jerk and his dead mind jump back to life. "Sal." He turned his eyes on her. His lips parted, a mouthful of questions yearning to be released. She pre-empted his thoughts.

"This is not the time for questions, Peter." And before he could contradict her stance she added, "We'll meet up after the funeral."

Her last word lingered hauntingly in his scattered mind—*funeral*—The mere word made him quiver inwardly. He hated funerals with a passion; avoided them like the plague and now—

He stared unblinkingly at the dark hole beneath, soon to claim his mother for all eternity, while he was counting down the days of his own miserable existence; his eyes lingering on the shiny brass plaque sparkling in the morning sun. Soon, he concluded, it would be covered up by clods of the earth; soon the casket, with his beloved mother inside, would be taken from view forever; soon Emily Brooke would be a memory.

Withdrawing his watery eyes from his mother's coffin, he looked around the small gathering of mourners. One particular man was not there, Peter noticed with relief; the man who had destroyed his mother's life.

"Come on, Peter." He felt the comforting hand lightly touch his arm and allowed Sally to usher him out of the cemetery.

After the last mourners had left, Sally patted the sofa invitingly. "Peter, we have a lot of things to discuss."

He sat by her side, turning his questioning eyes on her, feeling the unenviable link they shared. "How much do you know, Sal?"

"I know everything, Peter," she replied calmly, softly. "I dabbled in alcohol myself. Your mum had been my sponsor. We shared parts of our lives." She patted his hand comfortingly, feeling the protruding bones.

Minutes ticked away as they sat shrouded in silence; lost in a world they both shared briefly; when out of abandonment they had both found each other. Finally, Sally broke the spell, "I am going to look after you, brother because Peter, that's what you are to me and the closest I'll get to a real brother."

Her words filtered into his consciousness, but before he could say anything, she added, "And there will be no arguments, I'm moving into your pad."

As her presence grew stronger, his resolve grew weaker; both were secretly relieved that they had found each other once more; both, like last time were aware that their time together would be brief before, this time, Peter would be taken away forever.

There were lots of things to accomplish in the interim; a will to be, once again, carefully scrutinised; plans for his estate and wealth to be confirmed and his funeral to be thought about.

Sally cooked, cleaned and made Peter comfortable. They laughed, cried and hugged but most importantly, she listened very attentively to his instructions, making fervent promises to uphold his wishes, no matter how bizarre. She did not question or contradict. It was, she concluded, his call and his call only.

Sarah

She flicked on her bedside lamp and peered at the luminous hands of the clock; three-fifteen. She had been tossing and turning for over three hours; Peter Brooke's image bombarding her head mercilessly, until she felt her saturated head about to explode and the fragmented pieces of his haunting guise growing larger, amalgamating and creating a vivid symbol of her betrayal to a desperate, dying man.

Roughly throwing the duvet to one side, she slipped on her slippers and nightgown and sauntered downstairs into the eerily silent kitchen where she stood, her exhausted eyes staring starkly at the closed doors of a kitchen cupboard, goose pimples invading her arms beneath their soft, velvet covering. She could feel him on her arms, invading the whole of her body; his image swimming around and around in her head growing larger, clearer; invasive like an aggressive cancer; like the cancer he had, now attacking her from all sides. Robotically, she sat down her eyes staring—staring—*He's in there.* A voice whispered its volume growing. *He's in there—He's in there—He's in there—* Squeezing her eyes tightly, she tried to obliterate him from her mind. He's in there! Peter Brooke is in that cupboard—You owe him—You betrayed him—You betrayed a dying man—He's in there—He's in there—

Shaking her head from side to side, she willed the image of his desperately thin body, ravaged by the merciless disease, to go away; to disappear; to die. It loomed larger and larger; thinner and thinner; clearer and clearer. Her fingers grabbed the kitchen cupboard handle and flung the door wide open, making it bang against an adjoining door. Digging trembling fingers in, they curled around a package, her heart simultaneously turning into a block of ice. Abruptly her fingers withdrew and banged the door shut tight.

She sat and stared at his temporary tomb, the regular ticking of the clock mismatching her own irregular heartbeats, while a fresh bout of goose bumps invaded her trembling body once more, bringing with them a heavy wave of incredulity.

Slowly—slowly she felt her weak and trembling body drowning beneath a powerful wave—slowly—slowly the suffocating wave of a dead man's ashes, and his promise of revenge beyond the confines of death, overtook her... *Let our daughter be an everlasting reminder of your betrayal to a dying man...*

Her feet felt as heavy as two blocks of lead, she entered the bowels of the nursery and sat in an easy chair, the semi-darkness like a comforting blanket enveloping her, in her mind's-eye seeing only her daughter; Peter's daughter.

She gazed unblinkingly as if hypnotised, as the small bundle rose and fell in rhythm with her breathing; rising and falling—rising and falling like the undulating waves of a mighty ocean; rising and falling—rising and falling— breathing—living; a part of her; a part of—She closed her eyes tightly, obliterating from view the innocent lie beneath her; obliterating Peter Brooke's memory; obliterating the promise she did not fulfil to a dying man; the promise which was small fry compared to the precious gift he had given her.

She squeezed her eyes tighter; tighter still, her brain going back—back— back—If only she had told Brian the whole truth, her marriage would have been saved. She would still have her son. If only—

The iced blade which had plunged deep into her heart, the day Brian had slammed the door on their marriage and had turned away from her betrayal, with their son in tow, now twisted raggedly; the painful wound reopening wide and allowing a fresh bout of raw, undiluted pain to seep inside, while the clock ticked faithfully on, a witness to everything.

The first light of day started to filter through the curtain as she sat, her eyes on the child as ominous thoughts seeped into Sarah's head, making her eyes open wide. One day, she mused, Hope would know everything; one day she would know about her mother's shameful, deceitful ways; one day, she too, would disown her. Peter Brooke had seen to that.

Exiting the room, she re-entered the kitchen, threw wide open the unit doors and withdrew the shiny urn from its crumpled packaging, her fingers picking up two pieces of paper. As quickly as her trembling fingers would allow, she unfolded the first note and read it in its entirety, her eyes stopping on one sentence... *Our daughter will also have a part of me, to be given to her in a specially made locket on her thirteenth birthday...*

Eyes darted to the urn, a thought weaving deviously in Sarah's head. So much could happen in thirteen years; so many lies and half-baked truths; so many details could be added and omitted; so many—The shrill cry crashed into her thoughts, summoning her out of her disingenuous reverie. Holding the warm crying bundle close to her chest, she sat rocking to and fro, to and fro, as the warmth exuding from the infant seemed to wrap itself around her very heart and soul, bringing with it a unique kind of serenity as she continued to rock the infant back and forth, Peter's unsolicited image crashing into her calm mind as she drifted back—back—back to the first ever time she set eyes on him… *It was her friend's hen party and the small pub was already bursting at the seams with a motley assortment of revellers when they sauntered and fell in…*

Her eyes closed, as she felt the same rise of hot embarrassment she experienced all those years ago…*the stripper, in the guise of a policeman, walked confidently in waving his truncheon; she rushed out straight into her first encounter with Peter Brooke…* And then…*the wedding…the little white pills giving her false confidence and giving Peter a false impression.* Finally…*the hospital…the promises made…the ultimate betrayal…the baby…her husband and son long gone… Peter Brooke…* Or, at least part of him ensconced inside the confines of the shiny urn, now resting on her kitchen table. It was, she thought, like some sort of horror story or a dark comedy. Whatever it was, she concluded, it seemed surreal; not happening to her.

Her eyes dropped to her daughter and closed. It was not a fantasy. It was all too real and it was happening here and now and what she did, or did not do, would affect Hope.

An involuntary, ragged sigh escaped her mouth; if only Brian hadn't been shooting blanks. Her mind drifted, rolling back the time to her doomed encounter with Peter and her stark words… *I can give you comfort in your darkest hours; you, in return, can give me a baby…* Her watery eyes now lingered on the child he had given her; a hard, bitter lump rising to her throat making her eyes shift to the urn. "Where was I in your darkest hours?" She whispered. "Where was I?"

Sitting at the kitchen table, Hope wrapped securely in her arms, her eyes drifted to the printed card and picking it up she scrutinised it. *Memorial service for the late Peter Brooke. Saint Sebastian's church. 10 November. 10.30 a.m. Followed by the interment of ashes at Laceby cemetery.* Eyes flitted back to her daughter. "He was your daddy," she said softly into her fine hair, feeling the raw pain caused by her self-inflicted actions, as she rocked the child back and forth— back and forth.

Emma

Eyes glared at the printed card taking in the bold printed words. *Memorial service for the late Peter Brooke. Saint Sebastian's church. 10 November. 10.30. Followed by interment of ashes at Laceby cemetery…* Tossing the black-edged card onto the table, her fingers picked up the note, her eyes scanning the words… *Keep flirting, Emm. It suits your character…* Closing her eyes tight, she asked herself if that was what she ultimately amounted to being; a flirt; a tease; someone no one took seriously; a good-time girl flirting with any old Tom, Dick or Harry? Was that the lasting impression Peter had of her? As if by magic, all the men she had flirted with, that she could remember, came into sharp focus. Where were they all now? Her eyes drifted to the urn resting on the table. "And what the heck was you all about, Peter?" She asked aloud as an image of him, alive and well, popped into her head.

"Another flirt," she answered her own question. "And two wrongs never make a right."

One by one, the men she briefly dated paraded through her head and one by one they marched out, not one leaving a lasting, solid impression. How could they? She asked herself. They never stood a chance. I was too busy thinking about the next conquest.

Suddenly she felt trapped, enshrined in a tomb of loneliness. Where was the lovely detached house, with the five bedrooms she had once dreamed about? Where were the elegant garden, the three children and the dog? Where was the loving warmth and security of a faithful husband's arms around her? Where was the husband? The bleak eyes stared at the shiny urn, her soul as dead and lifeless as the ashes of the man she once unashamedly flirted with.

Eyes fixated on the container before her, she saw only her past; a life of laughter, casual relationships amounting to nothing, endless shopping sprees, a succession of pampering sessions, expensive holidays and spending money as if there was no tomorrow, as far as she was concerned, there was no tomorrow. Life was for today; the present; the here and now and sod tomorrow; sod husbands; sod children; sod the future. It was *now* that mattered and nothing else; or, so she thought.

As she stared unblinkingly at the urn, a cold wave of reality washed over her. Was this, she asked herself, what it all boiled, or rather burned, down to? Was this it? She closed her eyes. Where were the guys she had flirted with, the guys she had casually dated, where were they all? Opening her eyes, she glared disdainfully at the shiny mahogany container. "Where the fuck are you all?" She asked aloud.

He's in there, a little voice in her head whispered. *The guy who loved you, cared for you, wanted a chance with you; he's in there.* Unwaveringly, she continued to stare, her eyes glassing over. He's dead, she silently stated. *But he could have been somebody in your life if you had given him a chance.* The voice counteracted. No. She shook her head slowly from side to side. I didn't give him a chance. *You didn't give anyone a chance, except your self-seeking self.* The voice persisted now louder, firmer, clearer in her head. I gave Fluffball a chance. The voice laughed raucously. *You gave a dog a chance—you gave a dog a chance—you gave a dog a chance—*The voice grew louder and louder; louder and louder until she felt her head was about to explode. A dog can't hurt me—a dog can't hurt me, she repeated over and over again, salty tears spilling from her glassy eyes. *But you didn't give anyone else a chance.* The faint, almost inaudible, voice whispered. Moments passed; cold, silent, long and torturous minutes. "No," she stated aloud, "I didn't give anyone a chance."

Rising, she placed the urn back into its package and shoved it into the depths of the cupboard once more, placing the printed memorial card onto the mantelpiece. "I shall go to your memorial, Peter," she said aloud, "and then I shall start to learn how to love."

Tracy And Jade

Two pairs of eyes looked down at the ominous package which Jade was holding, as the *click-click-click* of stilettos echoed in both their heads.

"What is it, Jade?" Tracy peered at the brown crinkled paper, raising her bewildered eyes to her friend's shrugging shoulders.

"I haven't got a clue," replied Jade, as both women stared at the retreating woman walking down the short drive.

"Who is she?" Tracy continued questioning.

"No idea."

"Are you expecting anything?"

"No, are you?"

"No."

Two pairs of puzzled eyes swept back to the mysterious package.

Curiosity, as always, bubbled up in Tracy. Grabbing the package, roughly she tore the paper away, gasped and dropped the item onto the table gasping, "Oh God…oh God…"

Jade's eyes widened like saucers. "What the heck is it, Tracy?"

Seconds later, sitting rigidly in their chairs, they stared starkly at the solid, shiny mahogany container, an icy tomb-like silence shrouding them as they continued to glare and their stomachs churned. Finally, Tracy squeezed the words out of her bone-dry mouth. "It's…it's an urn, Jade." Vomit rose to her parched throat, as a pair of transfixed eyes stared at her.

Slowly Jade's trembling fingers gingerly touched the urn, her eyes once again darting to Tracy's stark eyes. "Who…who is dead?"

The chair scraped across the tiled floor, the urn was lifted and placed onto the window sill. "It's someone's idea of a sick joke, Jade."

"It's a bit late for Halloween."

"Only a couple of days." Tracy grabbed the brown paper, about to throw it in the bin, her eyes spotting a piece of paper.

Jade took the note out of her friend's trembling fingers, unfolded it and gasped, her shocked eyes flitting intermittently between the note and her friend's stunned face. "It's from Peter Brooke," she stated as she watched the colour drain from her friend's face.

"Read it," urged Tracy, her eyes glued to the fluttering paper Jade was holding.

Jade took a deep breath and began, "A brief note from the grave." Jade's racing heart suddenly stopped momentarily before resuming its rapid beat. "A brief note from the grave, so to speak, to two wonderful ladies, I barely knew, but have never forgotten for, without knowing it, you taught me the value of true friendship; something, which I admit, have never experienced. You taught me that nothing or, perhaps more importantly, no one should ever come between two friends. I tried and failed miserably but, in the midst of my destructive process, I learned that true fidelity is all about truth, honesty, loyalty, kindness, sincerity and respect; all these things I have tried to subsequently work on. I was the proverbial thorn which almost tore your friendship apart. Please forgive me and please remember, when you ever look at a rose, your friendship can exceed the pain of any thorn. Peter."

The heavy silence was penetrated by Tracy's soft words, "I was jealous, Jade."

Her friend turned, a whimsical smile pinned on her face. "And I didn't give him a chance." Her eyes espied something white amongst the crumpled packaging. Picking it up, she read, "Memorial service for the late Peter Brooke. Saint Sebastian's church. 10 November at 10.30 a.m. Followed by interment of ashes at Laceby cemetery."

Simultaneously, two pairs of eyes darted to the polished urn on the window sill. "I'll be there." Both women stated in unison and smiled at each other.

Mary

Once the initial shock of Peter Brooke's demise had rippled through her consciousness and registered in her mind, her sad eyes remained firmly fixed on the shiny mahogany urn, as scattered thoughts drifted in and out of Mary's head and finally took hold of her, bringing with them a mixture of smiles and fears. If only our worlds had not been poles apart. She shook her head regretfully, remembering the small bunch of colourful sweet peas he had given her; remembering the electric current surging through her as he touched her hand with his fingers; his kindness coming to the forefront of her memories. Her lips broke into a new smile, as she remembered the colour he always brought to her cheeks; the nice compliments he always paid her; remembering his kiss as an involuntary image crashed into her mind. Was it her loyalty to her dead fiancé that had prevented her from loving again? Was it because of him that she had not allowed Peter to claim her for his own, or was it the fear of loss? She closed her eyes. "It was never to be," she said softly, the details of Peter Brooke's scheduled memorial firmly etched in her brain.

Tommy

Old but never forgotten resentment rose like vomit to his throat making it tight, his guts twisted and wrenched, his pained heart felt once more the deep thrust of betrayal, as his cold eyes stared at the object in front of him; his lips set in a thin, unforgiving line as a surge of tsunami waves of bitter, undiluted anger overtook him wave by wave until he could feel nothing but raw hate for the man that was once his best friend.

Closing his eyes against the shiny, smooth surface of the urn, his mind drifted… They had been the very best of friends, more like close brothers than mates, he mused. Someone he had trusted with his life until—until… The blade in his heart plunged deeper propelling him to abruptly rise, take hold of the offensive object and bury it deep into the inner depths of the wall unit. Out of sight, out of mind, he told himself firmly, his eyes espying an envelope on the floor. Picking it up and turning it over, his heart turned to ice as his eyes stuck on five words staring up at him. *To my best friend, Tommy.* His guts immediately curdled with a new bout of raw, seething bitterness; his eyes closed to the personal affront on the envelope in his hands, making his fingers burn and throw the item onto the kitchen table.

The beer at *Bruno's* did not quell his agitated spirit. Four beers and a double whisky followed, heightening his agitation to fever point, making his blood surge and boil, his guts twist mercilessly, his head swim with thoughts of Peter Brooke, his so-called best friend and his beloved fiancée, Meredith… *Meredith—Meredith—Meredith…* The only girl he had ever truly loved; the girl who had been selfishly snatched away from him by Peter Brooke. "Another neat whisky; a double," he snapped at the barmaid, his seething eyes on fire.

Staggering out of the crowded pub, his wobbly feet somehow got him home, where he immediately retrieved the urn, poured himself a generous measure of neat brandy and sat staring at the container before him, his heart full to the brim with a mixture of hate and anger.

The minutes ticked laboriously on, as he brought the amber-filled glass to his needy lips and took a long swallow, his body momentarily shaking involuntarily from the instant effect of the rawness, while his unblinking eyes stared at the object of his scorn, diverting briefly to the sealed envelope propped in front of the urn, his pained heart beating heavily.

Taking another generous swill, and another, his fingers reached out and picked up the envelope, roughly tearing the seal and withdrawing a folded piece of paper. Raising the glass to his lips, he swallowed the potent liquid bit by bit, feeling the rawness, diluted a little with his own saliva; feeling it slide down his throat, down his gullet and settle somewhere deep—deep, exuding a wave of warm comfort; a false comfort; but a comfort nevertheless.

Carefully unfolding the paper, his eyes scanned the neat handwriting and rested on the name. "Peter Brooke," he said aloud, "my infernal enemy." His guts twisted with a surge of renewed vigour, his heavy heart raced, his fingers crumpled up the note into a tight ball and threw it into the waste paper basket before they reclaimed the glass, his mouth swiftly emptying it of its contents. Striding across to the drinks cabinet he replenished his supply; his red-blotched, glassy eyes glaring unblinkingly at the paper-ball.

Refilled glass in one hand, creased paper in the other, and Tommy's eyes dropped to the sentence of the first line and he began to silently read.

'Dear Tommy, the best buddy I ever had.

His guts creased like the paper in his hand but he read on.

I am sorry, Tommy.'

Widened, shocked eyes glared at the twelve words staring up at him and he shook his incredulous head from side to side. Twelve fucking words from a dead man, stating he was sorry. No plea for forgiveness; no explanation as to what propelled him to do what he did; just twelve words merely stating he was sorry.

He took a swig and squeezed his eyes tightly. It was as if the fucker had absolved himself. Tommy continued to shake his incredulous head, his fingers crumpling tight the paper and throwing it back into the basket, as his furious eyes darted to the black-edged printed card. Replenishing his glass once more, he staggered up the stairs, spilling drops en route to his bedroom, and fell onto his bed fully clothed.

Distorted images flitted in and out of his fragmented slumber… Meredith's happy eyes—Peter, his best mate, stabbing him in the back, taking his girl away from him and impregnating her with his sperm—Peter, his loyal friend; the betrayer; his worst enemy… His eyes shot open, and still, he could see Peter's deceitful smile, his roving eyes and his evil, rotten heart. Peter; the friend who had snatched away his Meredith; his future wife; his children; the happy years and gave him back nothing in return but heartache, loneliness and a heavy burden of mistrust.

He lay stark-eyed staring at the dull, pale ceiling above.

The small ancient church was full to bursting. The musty smell filled every nostril, covering the motley congregation with a stifling mantle, which bore heavily on each individual.

Stark eyes stared ahead as a young altar boy placed a heavy tome onto a stand, adjusted a page and exited into the sacristy. He re-emerged a few minutes later and proceeded to light the tall, erect candles one by one bringing a spark of life to the gloomy surroundings.

Hearts beat heavily beneath thick overcoats and woollen jackets; memories which were dead and buried, resurrected with the arrival of an unexpected, unwanted gift, hurling the unsuspecting recipients back into the past, they would have rather have left in the past; for, each individual had allowed Peter to enter his/her life and each had suffered the devastating consequences; a few had never recovered.

Mary Simpson's watery eyes stared unblinkingly at the stark cross on the altar, from which she derived no comfort; only cold, heavy emptiness. This was not how it was supposed to have ended. She snapped her eyes shut to obliterate the cross. Her God had failed her. Her fervent prayers had not been answered.

Briefly, she allowed herself to sink into comforting darkness before that was cruelly snatched away from her too. Unwanted thoughts crashed mercilessly into her head… *She was standing at the brink of an open grave…her glassy eyes registering, but unable to identify, the figure…* And now she was stood in the small church, one among many, with a scattering of Peter's ashes in a small container, in the depths of her pocket, as she had thought it the appropriate thing to do.

Eyes fixed on the vicar's mouth as he greeted his flock, she wondered what on earth had possessed her to come, her eyes shifting from the young man in the black garb and sweeping over the designer-clad mourners, telling her in no uncertain terms that she did not belong; she was not one of them for they seemed detached, worldly, out of reach. Her eyes returned to the vicar, her ears closed to his words; her mind, once more, drifting back to another time; to the precise moment she had determined to wait for him, words seeping out of her mouth, "You never came back."

She felt eyes shoot in her direction, jerking her out of her dismal reverie; her face feeling like a red-hot furnace, realising words had inadvertently escaped her mouth her eyes dropping to the pew in front, staring unblinkingly at a black mark ingrained in the wood. The faintest of smiles played on the corner of her mouth. *But, you did come back, Peter.* She closed her eyes, her cold fingers grasping the container in her pocket. *You did come back.*

A woman attired in a smart black designer suit, her skirt well above her knees, sat next to her current beau of two days, her eyes starkly set on the young vicar thinking, You're far too for dishy for this job, mate; you're wasted here. Licking her upper lip, she wondered what on earth had propelled him into the religious life; thinking about the things she could do with and to him if she was given half a chance.

Peter Brooke gate-crashed her colourful scenarios, forcing her thoughts to change their course of direction; his words, as clear as day, seeping into her mind... *You're a tease, Emma, and that about sums you up...* Eyes flitted to the guy standing by her side, darted back to the altar, dropped and rested on the shiny dark urn placed directly in front, her lips breaking into a knowing smirk. *You knew me well, Peter.* Her eyes darted back to her beau faithfully standing beside her, waiting for any crumb of attention she may throw his way. Eyes scrutinised his lean face noticing the involuntary twitch in his cheek, his black sleek hair swept to one side, and his dark eyes as they slid onto her. Aware of being observed her heart somersaulted. Maybe, she mused, she should make a go of it this time; maybe—Her eyes darted back to the urn. *Thank you, Peter,* her silent lips mouthed.

Two women dressed in black stood side by side, wondering what had possessed them to attend this memorial, commemorating the life of a guy they barely knew; a guy who had casually wandered in and out of their lives, leaving in his wake debris of emotional chaos and a shedload of uncertainty, which his sexual greed had brought to their friendship; a guy who had rocked their stable boat and stirred feelings neither knew they had for each other creating in both women a deep mistrust of all men, as their own bond grew and matured until they subsequently became an item, which inevitably excluded all men.

Stark eyes staring at the mahogany receptacle came to one conclusion; if it hadn't been for Peter Brook—

Simultaneously, as if each knew the other's thoughts, they turned their eyes away from the urn and onto each other; their mutual warm smiles secretly telling each other everything, before they turned their eyes back to the urn and thanked their benefactor.

Heavy solidified feet stood at the entrance, as eyes looked into the gloomy bowels of the ancient church, sweeping across the backs of black-attired bodies; across blonde, brunettes, redheads, bald heads, the odd spiky creation and finally resting on a distant object in front of the altar. A heart beat erratically, fingers clutched tightly, guts squeezed into a hard ball; feet reluctant to move a centimetre, unable to turn and run in the opposite direction; glued to the spot, as the haunting words of a mournful hymn drifted into her consciousness and a jagged blade thrust deep into the depths of her heavy, suffocating heart… *Abide with me*… The words wrapped themselves around her sad heart, her brain, her guts, her whole body and soul.

Involuntarily she moved. One step—two steps—three—four—five—step by step she moved forward, conscious of eyes watching her every move until her grateful eyes found an empty place where she perched, an unwilling prisoner. She shrivelled, retreated within herself like a snail within its shell, while layer after layer of Peter Brooke's world was peeling away and the haunting words of the hymn continued to permeate her soul.

Closing her eyes tightly a heavy, jagged sigh exuded from her lips, making the middle-aged woman next to her look sideways… *Abide with me*…her guts twisted mercilessly…*Abide with me*…her heartbeat laboriously…*Abide with me*…his body lay on the bed, gripped by the bony fingers of impending death. Alone, lonely and betrayed he lay, while she rejoiced in the selfless gift he had given her… *Abide with me*…her leaden heart stopped beating. His body lay still, abandoned; dead.

The solemn singing faded into a natural end; her eyes remained closed, allowing the momentary still silence to envelope her; denying Peter's image further access; feeling only the tendrils of her own betrayal to sink deeper and penetrate further the very depths of her conscious mind. Her eyes opened and switched to the framed picture beside the urn. Unable to see clearly, his image was alive and well in her head as… *His green observant eyes looked down on her as she asked herself, why am I like this; why can't I enjoy myself like the rest of them; why do I have to be different? ...and his strong voice stated, Different is good... You know, talking to oneself might be construed as the first signs of lunacy...* Now, shaking her head from side to side. she silently admitted that she must have, indeed, been a lunatic, to have engaged in any form of communication with the likes of Peter Brooke. A second heavy sigh escaped her mouth, her eyes desperately trying to focus on the vicar, the altar boys, the flowers; the cross above the altar; to focus on anything except Peter Brooke.

Her mind refused to obey as it wandered into forbidden territory... *May I have the pleasure? He extended both his hands in an invitation to dance and waited. Her startled eyes rose past his inviting hands to his resolute chin and lingered on his warm smile; moving further they rested on his eyes, which seemed to see into the very depths of her soul...* He swam before her eyes as did the ancient crumbling walls, the congregation, the vicar, the urn; all misted, blurred and blended into one and she felt her legs turn to jelly, as her heart beat erratically on, her mind drifting once more... *Well? ... I—erm—no—erm. Come on, Miss Indecisive...* Miss Indecisive—Miss Indecisive—The words grew louder and louder in her ears—*Miss Indecisive!* They shouted. Indecisive you were not, shouted back a loud, clear voice. Indecisive you were not when you asked Peter Brooke to give you his sperm; indecisive you were not when you agreed to his dying request; indecisive you were not, when you denied a dying man his last wish, to die with the comfort of knowing you would be there at the end; indecisive, Sarah Lisle, you most definitely were not!

Her watery eyes darted back to the urn, her heart feeling the sharp, unrelenting thrust of a blade.

... It's Peter; Peter Brooke. The years had taken their toll on him, she had thought. In fact, they had not been kind to him at all, she had silently assessed. He was a shadow of the handsome, self-assured man she had remembered. Now, he looked tired and haggard; his green, vibrant eyes had lost their sparkle and were full of pain... His words thrust the blade deeper into the raw muscle of her heart... *I am a dying man, Sarah...* And the sharp-pointed blade ripped through her heart, thrusting through her values and ethics; her responsibility, loyalty and sense of duty; ruthlessly lacerating them all into tiny, jagged fragments, making every dimension of her life nonsensical; making all things permissible. The knife plunged deeper as her own stark words cut through the very core of her conscience... *I can give you comfort in your darkest hours...*

And though the last words of *Abide with me* had seeped into the ancient walls of the church, they were ringing loudly and clearly in her head; accusing, damning, admonishing, until they whirled round and round and round, making her guts wrench mercilessly, her heart pound and beads of moisture to spring on to her forehead; forcing her feet to scramble out on to the aisle and walk briskly, breaking out into a run and running out of the stifling church, through the lychgate and on to the crunchy gravel, where her feet came to a standstill.

The opening words of, *God of Mercy and Compassion,* drifted eerily into her consciousness, making her tightly squeeze her eyes. If only I had a grain of faith, she shook her head dismally.

Crunch—crunch—crunch—she placed one firm foot in front of the other, the sound of rough gravel bringing a strange grain of comfort to her tortured soul, for it was the only thing that sounded real at this moment in time. Espying an old wooden bench, at the far side of the main body of the church, she rushed towards it, sat and stared into oblivion, from which she snatched sweet solace for, in the numbness of oblivion, she did not have to think.

Her sanctuary of oblivion did not wrap its walls of comfort around her for long, as thoughts of her betrayal, against the man who was being remembered on the other side of the wall, crashed into her safe haven. Memories of broken promises and betrayal flashed through her mind, promising fervently they would always haunt her; they would always be a part of her, a part of her past, her present and her future and the future of her child; Peter Brooke's child; his precious gift to her; a gift which had never been reciprocated.

Memories swam before her eyes, as the dulcet sounds of the hymn drifted out of the open window, the soothing lyrics doing nothing to quell her tortured soul as time, like the layers of an onion, peeled away; day after day; month after month—

The tolling of the bell shook her back to the present and, with the sharp stab of ruthless reality, came a decision propelling her to say aloud, "I will tell my child, Peter's child, everything." Rising, she walked back into the confines of the church.

Like two stones, numb and perfectly still they sat; two people sitting on either side of a third person and all three wishing they were anywhere in the world but not in Saint Bartholemew's, mourning for a man they did not care to mourn.

The woman's eyes dropped to her black, leather-gloved hands, where she felt the comforting support of her husband's hand, her eyes shifting to her son, her heart tearing in two… *Is it moon dust, Mummy?* … His innocent words filtered through time and yet they were as clear in her head now as if they had been spoken a mere second ago. She closed her eyes against the hot tears pricking her eyes. If only it had been moon dust… *It is your father—your father—father— father…* The cold, detached words echoed repeatedly in her head, as the prickly tears seeped out from beneath their lids, creating two dewy pathways along her cheeks and leaving her with a surging pain; feeling the protective hand tighten its grip, her husband feeling her pain.

"It's ok to cry, Meredith," he said so softly she barely heard.

Her whole body stiffened and her hand robotically withdrew from his swiftly brushing away the remnant of salty tears, feeling a wave of raw anger overtake her, making her want to scream, stamp and shout at the top of her voice. It's not ok—It's not ok, Frank—It's not fucking ok at all!

Her glazed eyes stared directly ahead, a fresh supply of bitter tears threatening to spill onto her pale, drawn face, as she saw her own betrayal of the only man she ever truly loved; the man who should be standing by her side, as she craved to obliterate Peter Brooke from her mind; erase him from her memory; forget he ever existed knowing full well, alive or dead, he would always play a part in her life.

As she stared past the framed photograph to some other time, she heard the echoes of a distant voice speak… *Let it go—let it go—let it go…* and not daring to shift her eyes for fear of revealing her emotions, she wondered whose words they were; Frank's, Johnny's, Tommy's or were they words spoken by a dead man. Or, perhaps, it was her own heart speaking to her… *Let it go—let it go—let it go…* The words reverberated softly, bringing with them a comforting serenity to her tortured heart… *Let it go—let it go…* And with the echoing words, the pain of her betrayal began to vanish—to disappear—to go. *It's time,* the voice in her head stated. *It is the right time.*

Glassy eyes shifted to the urn before the altar. It was time to let him go. Eyes darted to the frame; his smiling image in the picture echoing… *Let it go—let it go—let me go, Meredith…* She closed her eyes against his image.

Yes, her heart told her. It was time.

He stood alone in a crowded church, as old forgotten memories flashed in and out of his head, making his lips break out into a smile, changing rapidly into a frown, a grin; his eyes switching from sheens of sadness to sparkling veils, to observers of pain making him want to simultaneously laugh and cry out in frustration, anger and incredulity; to curse and forget in equal measures the man named, Peter Brooke; his old-time friend.

All eyes followed the slim, black-attired woman as she walked sedately down the aisle; paused briefly at the altar, lowered her eyes to the urn and made her way to the pulpit.

Sally Emery was not a figure accustomed to the skill of public speaking; neither did she revel in the prospect of being gawped at, and later gossiped about by a bunch of complete strangers, who she would probably never see in her life again. Determined to hold her ground, knowing her words would be under intense scrutiny, she drew comfort from the fact that Sally Emery never shirked away from responsibility and duty and now she had a job to do that only she could do and she had every intention of honouring the wishes of a dying man for, although she knew him briefly, Peter Brooke had been the closest person she had ever had in the world. She had felt she had grown to know him, for he had opened up to her in his last days and she treasured these days as if they were the rarest, most precious of jewels.

Her eyes scanned the motley congregation, identifying not one person. Not one meant anything to her; yet, she mused, they all meant something to Peter; they had all, in varying degrees, known Peter and, from the stories he had related to her, they had all played a part in his life; or, rather, he in theirs. She felt that without intrinsically knowing them, she knew about them to some degree; some better than others; others not so well at all and one or two, she felt, she knew quite intimately for Peter, in his more lucid days, had not held back on any details, much to her own embarrassment.

Her observant eyes had identified Mary straight away and immediately she understood the attraction Peter found in her, for behind the plainness, she assessed, there shone integrity, kindness, loyalty, love and weren't they the most important treasures in life?

Her eyes moved on to the two women sitting on the end of a pew. Tracy and Jade, she worked out as her eyes darted to the urn. *You should have known better than to have tried to come between those two lovebirds, Peter.* She shook her head, her eyes darting to Emma. *The flirt,* she silently concluded, her eyes swiftly moving on to Sarah where they rested, an inner anger rising. *A scheming Judas,* she declared silently, vehemently. Her roving eyes moved on to a small family and her heart numbed.

A cough jerked her out of her reverie, her eyes swiftly moving from Meredith and Johnny and on to the people sitting directly before her, attired in mourning black, her eyes rising to the vicar, whose questioning eyes were upon her as he repeated, "I believe you would like to say a few words, Miss Emery?" His eyebrows rose, forcing an array of horizontal creases to appear on his forehead, while Sally's heart and stomach joined forces and clenched tightly.

It was time to put the record straight. It was time for all to sit and listen to a man, friend or foe speak from beyond the restraints of death. Oh, how she wished now she had been brave enough to have refused his last request.

"Miss Emery," prompted the vicar standing at her side, "would you like to say a few words?"

The vicar's eyes seemed to bore into her very soul, his mild voice grate in her churning guts, as layer upon heavy layer of ominous silence wrapped itself around her waiting—waiting—for her to take the vicar's cue and honour the promise made to the man she called her brother. All eyes were upon her, making her shrink inwardly beneath their intense stares, making her heart pound and her feet itching to run.

Peter's weak, faltering words drifted into her consciousness... *You—you will—do—do this for me—won't you, Sally? You—you will keep—keep your pr...promise?* ... He grabbed her warm fingers into the enclosure of his bony hand... *Yes, of course, Peter... It will be done... It will be done...* Her words of assurance boomed in her head as she stood, like a solidified statue, her feet like clods unable to move, only her eyes shifted back to the clergyman, where she met a reassuring smile, silently telling her it was time to do her thing; to fulfil the promise she had made to a dying man, her brother.

A disturbing image of Sarah crashed into her mind. Peter's betrayer cast a moment of indecision, her feet ready to run. Forcibly banishing the image away, she hastily thrust her trembling fingers deep into her coat pocket, fumbled and retrieved a folded piece of paper which she placed, shakily onto the wooden lectern before her; her eyes rising and settling briefly on the expectant congregation, before they drifted from one individual to another, giving each a second of her time and her heart a chance to subdue its brutal beating. Dropping her eyes to the dark print of dictated words, she closed them briefly, praying furiously for sustained courage. She took a deep breath.

Eyes diverted from the page and rested on the black-grey blur of people before her as she said slowly, concisely, "These are the words Peter Brooke wished me to say to you at his memorial." Lowering her eyes, she began, her words faltering and weak at first, then slowly gathering momentum becoming stronger and clearer with each passing second.

A hard lump rose and lodged in her constricted throat, as she bravely fought back the tears, took a deep breath and continued to read Peter's words. "I am sorry, to each and every one of you gathered here, I am sorry for all the pain I have caused, in varying degrees. I was selfish, deceitful and arrogant. I was a flirt, a liar, a Judas and a despicable pig of a so-called man. In the end, if it's any grain of consolation to you, I feel I got my just dessert, for I am to die a lonely man. In my defence, I feel, I need to tell you that I loved you all in my own way; though, clearly and far too late, I realise, it was always the wrong way; the selfish way. I knew not how to love, or how to be loved and for those shortcomings, I truly apologise. Peter."

His name lingering on her lips, Sally proceeded to fold the paper, amidst the sounds of shuffling. Turning away from the lectern, she stopped, turned back, took a deep breath and stated in a firm, clear voice, "I am Sally and I was with Peter during the last days of his life. Peter told me everything, holding nothing back. He told me about his life, his loves, the women he hurt, the ones he impregnated and abandoned and the lost chances he had of being a father." Closing her eyes she took another deep breath, summoning up the confidence to say what she needed to say. "Peter was a good man." A contradictory laugh rumbled through the bowels of the church, making her eyes shoot up to the source of the laughter.

"Peter was a good man," she reiterated, "who did some pretty bad things which, in his defence, he has acknowledged. Perhaps," her eyes swept across the congregation, "perhaps some of his unsavoury deeds were due to his unbalanced upbringing for that, most certainly, was where his mistrust in people was rooted. His own biological father had walked out on him two days after he was born; his guardian abandoned him and the death of his beloved foster mother, Pauline, when he was at a tender age, hit him like a thunderbolt. He grew up mistrusting everyone, feeling that he had to snatch a grain of happiness where and with whom he could, no matter what the consequences. Unfortunately, his worst fear came to fruition anyway. Peter was a sad and lonely individual, who could not love for fear it would be cruelly snatched away from him and, therefore, he did not love." Her eyes left the motley crowd and darted to Peter's smiling photograph. "Sleep in peace, Peter," she said softly, turned her back on him and *click-clicked-clicked* up the aisle and out of the stuffy church.

Meredith

The clock on the wall ticked away the mindless seconds, as a black-attired woman watched her only child engrossed in a book; myriad different sentence openers erratically springing into her whirling mind and, just as abruptly, dying. The ominous ticking of the clock told her that time was of the essence; if she failed to capture the moment, her chance would be lost forever and the truth with it. Tears pierced her eyes, threatening to spill out and kill her resolve.

She looked deep into the innocent, puzzled eyes of her son, knowing he yearned to break free from her invisible clutches and escape into the outside world and the laughter of his friends.

"Johnny, I… I need to to…" She began falteringly, the flow of her words sticking to the palate of her mouth and struggling to make their exit.

His big eyes rested dormant on hers, his body fidgeting, restless to go, while his common sense told him to stay and listen to what his mum had to say; his head telling him it was going to be something serious. Why else, he asked himself, would she ask him to sit down and look at her? Frantically, he searched his mind, trying to remember if he had discarded his dirty laundry on the bedroom floor. A relieved smile spread onto his lips. He had popped it into the basket.

"Johnny," she repeated, watching his smile disappear as his words crashed into her consciousness.

"Are you feeling sad, Mummy because of my first daddy?"

A sharp-pointed blade thrust into her heart and broke it and, she knew, at that moment in time that the pain she felt would always be there; sometimes numbed; mostly raw, unrelenting, merciless. She nodded her head forcing a smile, her heart plunging further into the dark realms of the past as her son added, "Don't be sad, Mummy, he'll always be with us." He rose, scraping the chair against the wooden tiles. "Can I go now, Mummy?"

No! No! No! She yearned to shout at the top of her voice. No, you can't go. I have a thousand things to say; to explain; to apologise. No, you can't go! *Let it go.* Peter's resounding voice spoke from the grave, as she watched her son run out of the kitchen and into the innocent world outside.

The light tap on her shoulder made her jump, her eyes rising to a tall glass, three-quarters full of freshly squeezed orange juice, and rising further to the kindest loving eyes she ever wished to gaze upon. "Frank." Her acknowledgement of his presence was but a faint whisper on her lips.

Gazing lovingly at his wife he raised his glass of fruit juice. "Let's drink to Peter."

Hesitant for a second, she looked into her husband's forgiving eyes. "To Peter." Clinking her husband's glass with her own, she put down her glass, reached out for her husband's hand and placed it on her stomach, where they both felt the kick of their baby.

Mary

Mary stared at the claret in her glass and imagined the ruby-stoned engagement ring she never got to wear, on the third finger of her left hand. Taking a small sip, she savoured the dark fruit flavours in her mouth, before allowing the smooth liquid to slide down her throat. "He was a caring man," she stated aloud to the dark liquid in her glass, "a good man."

Like an invading army, Sally's words drummed loudly in her ears, mingled with distorted images of Peter Brooke's loves and the women he had impregnated and abandoned; the stark reality that she knew nothing about the man crashing mercilessly into her consciousness. But then, she concluded, he had entered and left her life in a blink of an eye. Bringing the glass up to her lips she took another sip, his stark words crashing into the forefront of her mind... *I knew not how to love... I am sorry... I knew not how to love,* her head moved from side to side, like a slow-moving pendulum, the words on her lips moving slowly, as she felt his lips on her lips. "You did know how to love, Peter; you just wouldn't give yourself the chance." Picking up the glass from the table, she swilled the remnants down her throat, placed the glass into the sink, switched the light off and walked up the stairs to her single bed.

Tracy And Jade

Jade and Tracy sat in their lounge, a glass of expensive bubbly in their hands and a half-empty champagne bottle resting briefly on the coffee table, as they reminisced about one man; the guest of honour at their private wake.

A black stiletto flipped into the air and crash-landed onto the highly polished wooden floor. "Ah, that's better," Tracy exuded a sigh of relief, as she tossed the other shoe into the air, raising her shapely, black-stocking legs onto the sofa and curling them beneath her, her hand stretching out for the bottle. Bringing the replenished glass up to her lips, she fixed her eyes on her friend and lover. "What did you think about the whole fiasco, Jade?"

Her friend swilled the remnants of her drink and abruptly stood up and straightened her all-too-short black skirt. "It was certainly an eye-opener which, I guess, puts certain aspects of his lousy character into perspective." Her loving eyes flicked to her lover. "Are you coming up, Tracy?"

"Yeah…in a while." Tracy's eyes followed Jade, as she walked out of the room and up the stairs, her thoughts drifting back to her brief fling with Peter Brooke. "You were a rat, Brooke," she stated aloud, after some moments of reflection; then, swilling down the bubbly in one full sweep, snapped the light off and raced upstairs to her waiting lover.

Sarah

Within thirty-five minutes of sitting down before a blank piece of paper, Sarah had completed her task, finding it was by far simpler to accomplish than she had initially anticipated and feared. In her neatest handwriting, she had merely written down the unvarnished truth.

In the morning, she had decided, she would start tracking Brian down. The truth had to come out.

Placing the note into a neatly addressed envelope, she popped it onto the mantelpiece and made her way to her bedroom. By the time she had switched off the light, her heavy-laden heart felt the tentacles of her betrayal loosening their grip.

Emma

A secret smile danced on Emma's lips as she cuddled up to her boyfriend, an involuntary chuckle breaking out and making the man sitting next to her look down, his brow furrowing in puzzlement. "What's up, Emma?" He asked, his questioning eyes focused on the woman he loved, as her inadvertent chuckle transformed into a hearty, uncontrollable laugh.

"It's—it's Peter," she managed to say in between further bouts of laughter.

"Peter?"

"Peter, the guy in the urn or, rather the bits of him in there; you know, a portion of his ashes." More chuckles escaped as she tried desperately to control herself, as an old scenario was now seen in a very different light.

"Come on, Emma; spill," urged Josh, wanting to share in the hilarity.

"Well…" Her glassy eyes flitted to Josh. "Well…" A fresh attack of giggles possessed her, gradually they became lighter, enabling her to still her laughter-raked body and focus her watery eyes on the man sitting by her side. "Well," she began, closing her eyes and stifling more unruly giggles, "to cut a long story short, Peter bought me a puppy one Christmas, and well, I ended up thinking more about Fluffball than I did Peter."

"Fluffball?" Josh raised a curious eyebrow.

"Fluffball, my puppy. Anyway, after Peter had died, an urn arrived on my doorstep, so to speak, and I thought it contained my Fluffball's ashes. I dropped the urn in shock, the ashes scattered and to this day, I am still searching for some of Fluffball's ashes. Had I known the true nature of things, I would have abandoned the search long ago."

In unison, they broke out in laughter before he took her in his arms and kissed her passionately, sweeping all thoughts of Peter, his ashes and Fluffball out of Emma's mind.

Sally

Sally stood at the graveside, her eyes staring starkly at the black marbled headstone; a shiny, mahogany urn held tightly in her hands. For long minutes she stood perfectly still, while a scattering of thoughts whirled around her head, making her wonder what kind of woman Emily, Peter's mother, really was.

By all accounts, she had been portrayed as a good, kind, caring woman; her downfall being that she had allowed her heart to rule her head, especially where that despicable guy, Malcolm, was concerned; a woman who had loved her only son, Peter; a woman who had made a wrong decision in life which, as a consequence, led to detrimental consequences for her only child.

A heavy, ragged sigh, coming from her heavy-laden heart, exited Sally's lips, making her close her eyes against the cold, solid marble before her; the ultimate symbol of death. If only things had been different; if only Malcolm had not entered the scene; if only—if only—

Malcolm; the name grated through every single raw nerve in her body; *Malcolm*, the man who had sent her own mother into a devastating spiral of despair; *Malcolm*, the animal who had made her own life a living hell. *Malcolm—Malcolm—Satan!*

Bitter, hot tears slid down her cold face, as torturous years in foster homes and orphanages swept by and became one; swirling, whirling years of abuse, both physical and mental; years of hunger and depravation; years of being tossed out of one home and placed into another—into another until, finally, she was placed in Uncle Damian and Auntie Rose's care, where her only consolation was finding Peter for, up until he had arrived, she thought, she was the only one in the whole wide world who had been cursed and forgotten.

After Peter's arrival, there was a flicker of hope, for in helping him in her own little ways, she began to gain confidence and, in gaining confidence, she gained an inner strength to escape out of her dismal world and find a ray of light; the core of her salvation; Peter.

She dropped her eyes to the urn clutched tightly in both hands, her heart clenching mercilessly beneath her heavy overcoat. Slowly, raising the lid, she peered *into* the dark depths, remembering her promise as his weak, faltering words hammered into her head… *Promise m…me, Sal…you will despatch…a bit of m…me to the ladies…*

A sudden thought struck her, her eyes glued to the urn as she said aloud, "If all the good fragments of your life had been moulded into one relationship, you would have made the lucky lady a very fine husband, Peter Brooke." A whimsical smile danced on her lips before her eyes flitted back to Emily's headstone and, tipping the urn, she scattered the ashes saying, "Where you belong, Peter, Mother and Son."